MASTER
of the
ART
of
DETECTION

Liese Sherwood-Fabre

Little Elm Press, LLC

ISBN: 978-1-952408-33-5

PRAISE FOR LIESE SHERWOOD-FABRE

Overall, Sherwood-Fabre's reimagining of the famous detective ably expands the possibilities of the Holmes canon. A multifaceted and convincing addition to Sherlock-ian lore.

—Kirkus Review

Sherwood-Fabre's attention to detail and vivid prose are on full display in this delightful look at the evolution of a young Sherlock Holmes.

—Book Life Prize

Crafted to perfection.

— Chanticleer Book Reviews

To Claudia Rose,
Friend and Mentor

CONTENTS

A classic mystery story involves "the locked room," where a crime is committed under seemingly impossible circumstances. A victim is discovered alone with all windows and doors locked. The perpetrators have no way to enter or leave following the crime. In the original Sherlock Holmes cases, these include "The Adventure of the Speckled Band," "The Adventure of the Empty House," and "The Adventure of the Norwood Builder." Here's my own take on one such crime.

THE ADVENTURE OF KISIN'S CURSE

The telegram arrived as we were finishing our dinner. I had already planned a stroll in the cool spring evening and considered the intrusion more than slightly annoying. My friend Sherlock Holmes was in high spirits, having recently completed the case of the singing blackbird, and had agreed to accompany me on my evening walk. Any time I could persuade him to take from his usual melancholy pursuits I considered a victory. Of course, the telegram from Scotland Yard requesting his assistance raised his spirits even more.

"What do you know about the Mayan civilization, Watson?" he asked and handed me the telegram.

"Central American, I believe," I said as I skimmed the missive requesting his assistance at the Explorations Club where a death had recently occurred. A frown threatened to pull my lips down as my plans for a stroll vanished with the delivery boy. Forcing more good humor into my tone than I felt, I added, "Why do you ask? I see no reference to them here."

He stepped to a bookshelf and pulled out one of his scrapbooks. "Lestrade doesn't have to. The address says it all. The club has recently gained quite a bit of notoriety following the publicity of their most prominent member, Sir James Brandon-Smythe."

"I recall reading about him," I said, rubbing my chin. "He received his knighthood for having discovered a temple, I believe."

"A temple of the god Kisin, the lord of the underworld." He flipped through the pages of his scrapbook and stabbed his finger on one item. "Here it is. 'Brandon-Smythe Displays Grisly Sacrifices Returned from Mayan Temple.' Apparently, he discovered some well-preserved mummified remains in the structure's foundation."

I read the article over his shoulder, studying the illustration that accompanied the piece. Although still annoyed, the man's work was intriguing. "Amazing that those items survived the climate there. He says it was due to their having been sealed in some sort of vault."

"The Mayans must have had advanced knowledge of preservation techniques," he said with a nod. "I should like to examine the pieces more closely. Imagine being able to maintain specimens...." After a brief reflection on this idea, he slapped the book shut and dropped it on the nearest chair. "Perhaps I shall request a small sample for some chemical analysis."

LESTRADE WAS WAITING for us at the entrance to the Explorations Club in the Pall Mall area. I stared at the unassuming building. It hardly seemed the gathering place of some of the most prestigious and daring adventurers. Just a simple white stone building with a large wooden door. Inside, however, it became apparent this was no common club. The hallway was filled with maps, game trophies, and glass cases of ancient and native artifacts conveyed from faraway places. Ordinarily such a display would have piqued my friend's interest but on this occasion, Holmes followed Lestrade with a deep intensity to the broken door frame halfway down the main hall where the dead man had been found. For myself, I had to keep my eyes straight ahead to avoid stopping and examining each case's content.

The good inspector provided a short commentary while we passed. "The man's name is Joseph York, Sir James' assistant. They had to break in to get at the poor chap."

At the door to one room, he consulted a small notebook while Holmes peered inside. "Winston, the butler, discovered the man had locked himself in, but Sir James demanded they break down the door. It's a sort of laboratory the club provided to store and examine the things he brought back from Central America. Between him, the doorman Davidson, and Winston, they were able to force open the door. Found him just like he is."

"And the men who broke in?" Holmes asked. He still stood in the doorway, his gaze moving around, most likely taking in every detail.

"My men are guarding them in the library. I assumed you'd want to interview them yourself. Sir James warned everyone not to touch anything in case whatever killed York could still be lethal. Said something about the curse of Kisin."

I stepped to the door to get my own view of the scene. The warning about something lethal made me think twice about breathing in the air, but the other men had survived. I assumed I would as well. The room did have the feel of a laboratory with several black-topped tables arranged in rows where specimens could be spread out. Only one was in use now. A series of thin papers covered in drawings were spread across its surface. Lining three walls were a series of cabinets displaying ancient Central American artifacts—arrows, pottery, and even a few shrunken heads. One cabinet to the far right of the tables stood open.

On one chest-high shelf, a clay pot lay on its side. A cluster of five short arrows protruded from the pot's open mouth, and a liquid dripped from it to the floor. Sir James' assistant, however, was not visible.

Holmes pulled a pair of leather gloves from his pocket. "I think I'll have a look about the room and the victim now. I would suggest you use your gloves as well, Watson. Until we determined what killed Mr. York."

He headed toward the open cabinet but stopped and disappeared behind a table in front of it. "I'd appreciate your medical opinion here, Watson."

"That's where Mr. York is," Lestrade whispered to me. "He's lying on the floor in front of that table."

With a hard swallow, I thrust my hands into my gloves and stepped into the room. The dead man lay on his side, his back to the door as if in repose. I knelt next to him and lifted one arm. It flopped back to the ground with a dull *thump*. "I need to see the man's face to check for rigor."

With as much care as we could, we turned the man onto his back. When we did so, the cause of death became very apparent. An arrow, similar to the ones still in the overturned pot, protruded from his chest. After peering at the man's features, I said, "Stiffness will indicate how long since death. I see no signs of rigor, suggesting this happened very recently."

"Is that all you observe?" he asked.

I picked up his hand. "No rigor here, either. His palms aren't calloused, and his nails are more groomed than mine. Researching ancient Mayan cultures doesn't appear to be a very dirty job."

He appeared not to have heard me because he pointed to a red spot on the man's collar. "What do you make of this, doctor?"

"There's a nick just above it on his neck. Must have cut himself shaving this morning and bled a little on the collar. Odd. As well-groomed as he is, I would have expected him to change it. He must not have noticed it."

Before I finished this comment, Holmes had already turned to an examination of the man's clothing. In the right jacket pocket, he found a key. He studied it and the broken door, then stored it in his waistcoat pocket. Rocking back on his heels, he took in the man from head to toe and then stood, moving to the cabinet.

He focused his attention first on the overturned pot. "There's some sort of primitive spring inside. It appears that the assistant may have disturbed the pot, and it ejected an arrow into his chest. Additional analysis is needed, but I would guess it is tipped with curare."

Curare.

The small hairs on the back of my neck twitched. The poison creates a slow death as it paralyzes the person by attacking the muscles. Death occurs when it reaches those affecting respiration. We had faced this particular toxin once before. When investigating a report of a vampire in Sussex, Holmes had uncovered an attempt to murder a child with the substance. While not successful in that case, the Mayan trap appeared more effective.

"If it is curare, then the time of death is earlier than I originally suspected. Unfortunately, the drug slows the onset of rigor," I said.

"I'm not sure how that bit of information would enlighten us," he mumbled, now surveying the cabinet's contents from a few feet in front of its open doors.

I pulled my chin back at the slight his words carried and couldn't keep all my indignation from my voice. "It would have helped to more clearly define when the accident happened."

"Perhaps," was another muttered response as he turned from the cabinet and made his way to the table holding the thin papers.

Despite my annoyance, I joined him there. My curiosity about what they held overcame the sting from his snub at my observation.

Up close, I saw they were rubbings like those done of names and dates on old gravestones. Only these were stylized figures. More blockish in nature than any carvings I'd seen.

"Fascinating," Holmes whispered. He removed his glove and ran a finger below the images copied there. "I believe these lie at the heart of Sir James' discoveries. I read they prove the site was a temple to Kisin and also chronicle how the Mayans built their temples. He concluded the civilization had domesticated horses and other beasts of burden and used them to drag the large stone blocks to the site."

Unable to make see how these crude drawings indicated anything, I pointed to a stack of large glass plates next to the tracings. "What are those?"

My friend picked up one and held it before a lamp. "They appear to be copies of the temple drawings. These can be projected onto a wall for presentation to an audience." He spun about to address Lestrade, who was still in the doorway. "I should like to speak to those in the library now."

THE TWO POLICE officers guarding the room stepped aside when we approached with Lestrade.

"Has anyone entered or left this room since they were dispatched here?" the inspector asked one.

The man stood at attention. "No, sir. They haven't even made much noise. It seems the scene froze their tongues."

"Let's hope they'll thaw a little for us," Holmes said.

As expected for a club dedicated to exploration, the library housed a multitude of books on the room's four walls but also included display cases like those in the hallway. Several globes topped different tables scattered about the room, and the wall space not lined with books held framed maps instead of the paintings or portraits common to such rooms. Wing-backed leather chairs were arranged in clusters around the tables to foster conversations between members, although, at present, the three men seated in chairs near the fireplace didn't seem in a very sociable mood.

They turned toward us when we entered. Even though I lacked Holmes' powers of perception, I could identify the butler Winston and the doorman Davidson from their uniforms. The third, dressed in a well-made, but ill-fitting, suit, I concluded, was Sir James. He had apparently lost a lot of weight recently.

As a physician, the appearance of all three concerned me. My first instinct was to check their pulse and order each a brandy. Their faces were still pale, suggesting they were still in the initial phases of shock.

Before I could make such a suggestion, Holmes asked, "Which one of you was the last to see York alive?"

Brandon-Smythe raised his hand. "I was. I planned to make a presentation to the club tomorrow and had York assisting in my preparations. He'd copied some of the temple drawings on glass so that I could project them onto a wall and was going to gather some of the objects for a display."

"When exactly did you see him?"

"About three o'clock." He shook his head and made a sort of *tsk-tsk* sound. "I told him to be careful with the items. They had to be handled delicately because the Mayans were known to set traps to keep thieves from stealing temple treasures. One of the workers at the temple site tripped something which severed his head from his body. The natives call it the curse of Kisin."

"He did warn us to be careful when we broke in. Said there might be traps," the doorman said.

Holmes turned to the man. "We'll get back to that point. I want to understand the sequence of events first." Returning his attention to the knight, he asked, "You say you left him at three o'clock. Did anyone see you leave?"

The other two exchanged glances before the butler Winston said, "We both did, sir. I was down the hall and heard Sir James take his leave of Mr. York. When he stepped into the hallway, he asked me to inform Davidson he would need a cab and said he was going to the kitchen to arrange that dinner be brought to Mr. York at six o'clock. I told him it was quite irregular to allow a non-member the use of the club's amenities, especially meals, without a member present."

As if aware of how the dispute might appear to others, Brandon-Smythe responded to the accusation before Holmes could frame his next question. "I assured Winston the club's board had provided a special status to York for his assistance in my preparations and that I would return around that time anyway. He left to order the cab, and I followed."

"And where did you go for those few hours?"

"I met with some of the sponsors of my original trip. They wanted an update on the research I will be presenting here at the club."

"And you returned...?

The knight glanced at the clock ticking over the mantle. "It's been about two hours now. So, a quarter past six."

The butler nodded. "Sir James sought me out to ask if I had served Mr. York his dinner. I explained that he hadn't responded to my knock and that the door was locked."

"That's when he came to the entrance and asked me if Mr. York had left. I assured him that I had not seen Mr. York since his arrival this morning," said the doorman.

"All this was highly irregular for York," said his employer. "He's a very meticulous person. That was one reason I had him copying the tracings onto the glass."

His remark made me chew on my mustache, trying to recall my brief examination of the man. I remembered his well-groomed nails. Had he worn gloves for the task? I would have to ask Holmes about it.

Brandon-Smythe continued, "I requested Davidson accompany us and assist in gaining access to the room."

"And there is no other key?" Holmes asked.

"That particular room was never locked in the past," said Winston. "We had only the one, which I passed to Sir James when he was given the room for cataloging his discoveries."

"We would regularly lock the room from the inside to avoid just the type of accident that befell York," said the explorer with another shake of his head. "I couldn't be responsible for someone else falling to Kisin's curse."

"And so, you three broke down the door." He puckered his lips before asking, "Did all of you go into the room?"

"When the door gave way, we sort of fell in. We didn't see Mr. York at first, him being on the floor and behind the table and all," said Davidson. "Sir James sent us to count the tracings. Said there should be twenty. He was afraid someone had tried to steal 'em."

Holmes listened, eyes down as if in thought. At this bit of information, he directed his attention to Davidson. "Who noticed Mr. York first, then?"

"Well," the doorman said, drawing out the vowel. "We went to the table, but before we could count 'em, Sir James gave a little yell, saying York's been hurt."

"We started toward him, but he pointed to the pot with the arrows and told us to get out of the room because there might be poison in the air or it might let another arrow fly," said Winston.

"And all of you left at the same time?"

The three nodded, and Davidson added, "I went outside and flagged down a passing officer. Told him what happened, and he said to stay away from the room, and we've been in here since Inspector Lestrade and the other officers came."

My friend paused, hands behind his back. He sucked a bit of air through puckered lips as if he were about to light his pipe, although he had none in his mouth, a clear sign he was deep in thought. What was it that puzzled him? The events seemed clear to me. York had opened the cabinet to retrieve something and hit the pot by accident, springing the arrow that pierced his chest. The poison brought on a slow death as his whole body paralyzed, suffocating him. The thought of the poor man's drawn-out demise sent a shiver down my spine. I'd read of experiments with the toxin. The victim remained conscious, fully aware of events with no loss of feeling, but unable to move. He might have been revived with the proper assistance, but with no one there and unable to call for help, he became the only witness to his own death.

My thoughts returned to the present when Holmes addressed Sir James. "I wonder if you would allow me to take a sample of the substance in the pot for analysis?"

The man's eyes rounded. "Do you think it safe? One scratch—"

"Yes," Holmes said slowly and continued more to himself than to anyone in the room, "One scratch...."

He spun on his heel and spoke to me over his shoulder. "Come with me, Watson. I may have need of your assistance. And Winston—" The man stiffened as if to attention. "Please be so kind as to supply me with a small flask or two to collect the sample."

I hesitated when we reached the broken doorframe, the small glass bottles the butler had passed me in my hands. "Are you sure it's safe?"

"Perfectly. Curare is only dangerous when administered under the skin. The South and Central American tribes use it for hunting, paralyzing their prey to kill it. They then consume the meat with no harmful effects, despite the drug in the animal's system. If we don't disturb any of the other items, there should be no issue."

As he spoke, Holmes made his way to the open cabinet. He studied the scene for a second time before requesting one of the flasks. "This pot's been moved. The dust on this self has been disturbed."

"Probably when York was getting something for the presentation."

"But what?" he asked, scanning the objects on that and the other shelves. "Once I collect these samples, we can return to Baker Street."

As we turned to leave the room, I gave York one last glance. Now on his back, his arms to his sides, he could almost have been asleep, except for the arrow rising from his blood-stained shirt. I dropped my eyes out of respect for the hapless victim of the ancient curse.

Before returning to our flat, Holmes stopped at the telegraph office to send off a few messages. He didn't share to whom or on what business, and I'd learned from practice my curiosity would be rewarded at some point. Once back in our residence, he moved to the chemistry equipment occupying one corner and spoke little except to request I inform Mrs. Hudson that any responses to his telegrams be brought to him immediately.

After completing this assignment, I retired to my bedroom.

He was still at it in the morning when I came to breakfast. My first action was to open the windows and let in some fresh air. "What have you been burning? It smells like…." I paused, unable to find the words to describe the terrible stench. "I may eat my breakfast in my room to keep from tasting whatever you've been incinerating."

"Ah, Watson," my flatmate said as he turned in my direction. He held a flask in one hand and was swirling the dark, murky liquid about in it. "You've arrived just in time. I've finished my analysis of the substance in the pot. In case of any doubt, I have definitively determined that it was curare. However, not potent enough to kill a man. Observe the bird on the table."

I gasped at the pile of yellow feathers at the bottom of the cage. "Good heavens. You've killed Mrs. Hudson's canary."

"Not killed, merely paralyzed." He glanced at his watch. "Another minute or two, he will rouse himself. If this formula won't kill a canary, it certainly wouldn't harm a man of thirteen stone. The replies to my telegrams arrived during the night as well. I have almost all I need to draw my conclusions."

As if on cue, the bird blinked its eyes, signaling a return of its faculties, but Holmes paid it no heed. Obviously deep in thought, he stared out the window. When he turned back, he seemed reanimated. "I need to go out for a consultation. I'll be back in a bit."

"But breakfast—?"

"No need for food at present. Dulls the mind. But, please, enjoy yours.

I will, however, ask you to have Mrs. Hudson prepare some coffee for when I return. In about…" He checked his watch. "Two hours should do it. Then we shall be heading back to the Explorations Club."

Once again, I put my patience to the test as I waited for his return. After I finished my breakfast, I tried to read from one of my latest medical journals but found my gaze drifting to the clock to check the time. When I'd read the same page for the fourth time, I gave up and simply stared out the window until a quarter to the second hour. At that time, I requested the coffee from Mrs. Hudson.

My friend returned in almost two hours to the minute. He was as animated as any hound before the hunt. He downed a cup of coffee from the pot Mrs. Hudson had provided, rubbed his hands together, and gave a self-satisfied smile. "I have it all now. Come along, Watson, they will be waiting for us at the club."

This announcement caused me to pause in the doorway. When Holmes had noted we would be returning to the club, I had assumed he wished to review the room a second time. I called down the stairway, where he waited for me by the entrance. "They? Who is this 'they' waiting for us?"

"Why Lestrade and the three men who found Brandon-Smythe's assistant. I already sent out the telegrams, requesting they be at the club at a quarter to. We must not keep them waiting."

While I would have liked to ask him just what he'd discovered, he was much too agitated and preoccupied to find my questions anything but an annoyance, so I kept my peace for a third time on this case, knowing that all would be answered shortly.

When once again we entered in the library where Sir James, Winston, and Davidson sat, I also noted Inspector Lestrade and two of his officers were there also.

The loss of his assistant had deeply affected Sir James. Not only did he wear a black mourning armband, he also seemed even more shrunken than he had the day before, as if grief had depleted him.

"I see you all received my invitations, and I thank you for responding. First, let me state that based on my investigation, I have concluded Mr. York was murdered."

The inspector drew in his breath. "Now see here, Mr. Holmes, you can't be makin' accusations like that without—"

"But I do, Lestrade. I have proof this was no accident. It was *made* to appear like one. We can be certain of the following: York opened the cabinet, disturbed a pot filled with curare-tipped arrows set to impale anyone lifting the lid, and was hit by an arrow. Sailors refer to this as a 'booby trap,' although Sir James calls it 'the curse of Kisin,' a myth meant to discourage intruders from desecrating the temple."

The inspector broke in again. "What makes you think it wasn't this curse?"

"Because of the anomalies. Of which there were many." He ticked them off on his fingers. "First, what was he retrieving from the cabinet? The only intact pot was the one with the arrows. All others were shards, pieces of pots. Furthermore, the pot with the arrows had been recently moved toward the cabinet's edge. Nothing else had been disturbed in the cabinet. He had nothing in his hands, nor did anything else show signs of being moved or fallen. Even more intriguing was the scratch on his neck. Initially, I thought he had simply nicked himself shaving, but it was too fresh for that. Furthermore, the curare in the pot was too weak to kill a grown man. My analysis and a telegram from one expert confirmed that the poison comes in different potencies, and this one would have paralyzed him, but not killed him. It wasn't even strong enough to kill a small bird."

The image of Mrs. Hudson's canary flitted through my brain, and then the realization that poor York had lain on the floor while someone....

"Good lord," I said. "The murderer stabbed him with the arrow? Into the heart?"

"Exactly, Watson. An injection of the poison directly into his heart accomplished what the scratch wouldn't. Having ensured his demise, the murderer arranged the scene to make it appear like an accident and left."

Winston glanced around at those in the room. "Who did that? You think one of us? I had no reason to harm the man. Besides, he'd locked himself in. You found the key in his pocket. And I heard Sir James conversing with him before he left."

My friend spun about to face him. "Did you? Hear a true conversation between Brandon-Smythe and York? Or did it just appear that Sir James was talking to someone?"

The butler paused, apparently recalling the events of the previous evening. He drew in a sharp breath. "You're right. Sir James said at the door he would arrange dinner for him, but I don't remember York replying."

At this pronouncement, the knight rose to his feet. "Now see here, I'll not listen to any more of these baseless accusations. The man York made a grave error by opening the cabinet and disturbing the pot."

He moved as if to leave, swaying slightly on his feet, but the two officers who had accompanied Lestrade stepped in front of the library door, effectively blocking the only exit. Holmes placed himself between the man and the officers and continued reciting his conclusions.

"You, sir, are the one who made the grave error. You set the pot on the edge of the cabinet shelf and instructed York to open the door to retrieve something from the cabinet. When he did so, the pot tipped over and released the arrow. It, however, almost completely missed the man, only scratching his neck. Enough to paralyze him, but not enough to kill him. You had to do this yourself."

"I'll not listen to any more of this-this fairy tale," he said and took a step toward the door.

With his next step, he swayed again, appearing unable to keep his equilibrium. Despite his stated desire to leave, he collapsed into the nearest chair. I made a move toward him, but the knight waved me off. "I don't need your help."

Lestrade frowned. "I do have one question of my own, Mr. Holmes. What about the key?"

"After discussing the dinner arrangements with Winston, Sir James sent him to request a cab. He merely locked the door before leaving the building. When he and the others broke in the door, he sent the others to count the tracings. While the two men were busy with this task, he slipped the key into York's pocket before the others saw the murdered man."

"Fiction, I tell you," Brandon-Smythe said, his face now turning a deep vermillion. "What possible reason would I have to harm the man—let alone murder him?"

"That is what puzzled me at the beginning. Not the *how*—I quickly deduced the sequence of events—but the *why*. The motive. Why murder an assistant who had never set foot outside of England, or London for that matter? If you wish to accuse someone of fairy tales, Sir James, I would look no further than yourself. All this poppycock about a Mayan curse. If such misfortune derived from the temple's desecration, you, sir, are the main desecrator and would be lying on the floor.

"No, the motive lay elsewhere. About five feet elsewhere. I sent a telegram last night to the country's foremost expert on South American flora and fauna as well as the authorities to learn more about the death of the worker you described. This morning I compared your tracings with similar temple carvings on display at the British museum. I determined three facts: there were no horses—or most species of cattle (the bison being the exception, of course)—in the Americas until the arrival of the Europeans. That the deceased worker was the victim of yellow fever. And apart from the aforementioned animals, Sir James' tracings bear a remarkable resemblance to those in the British museum. I confirmed the meticulous Mr. York had visited the museum and must have come to the same conclusions about the temple carvings. He must have presented this information to Sir James. The man had just been knighted because of his discoveries. He couldn't risk the scandal the truth would have caused."

Brandon-Smythe leaped from his seat, glanced around the room as if seeking a place to run, and literally crumpled to the floor, his legs unable to support him. The seven of us rushed forward to carry him to the nearest couch, although all of us weren't needed to do so. When I took his wrist to check his pulse, I found him to be only skin and bones.

I revived him with ammonia and brandy provided by Winston. A pale bit of color returned to the man's cheeks.

Once more aware of his surroundings, he muttered so softly, I had to bend forward to hear him. "What have I done? Poor York. I killed him. And for what?" He turned his head and focused on my friend, his voice a bit stronger. "You're right, of course, Mr. Holmes. I shouldn't have tried to fool you. Better to have accepted the shame than to take a man's life. I-I simply couldn't return with nothing to show for my work or to the trip's backers. Two years tramping through the jungle. The curse of Kisin," he sneered at the name. "Yellow fever was my curse. It killed one worker out right. I made up the story about his head. Sounded more dramatic. In my case, it caused a lingering illness that will be my death one day soon. I spent weeks shaking and sweating in a native's hut. When I recovered enough to leave, I bargained with those in his village for the trinkets you see in those cabinets."

I glanced at Holmes and Lestrade and shook my head. The shock of the exposure of his deceit and his weakened condition had taken its toll. The man was likely to be an invalid for the rest of his life, if he survived at all. "This man needs constant medical attention. He should be taken home and care arranged immediately."

After the carriage with Sir James disappeared around the corner, Holmes turned to Lestrade. "It is, of course, up to you whether to arrest the man or not, but I believe he is not long for this world. He will most likely not survive to be tried."

"Doesn't seem right, though," said the inspector as he tugged on his waistcoat, "not punishing him for taking another's life."

"I would say his punishment will come swiftly enough. Both he and his assistant have fallen to the curse of this Mayan god."

There are more than one hundred "untold" cases mentioned by Sherlock Holmes. Many were referenced by Holmes in his discussion with Dr. Watson. Some may have been written and stored in Watson's tin dispatch box he kept in a vault a Cox and Company. Among these is a reference to one in "The Sign of the Four." Holmes tells Watson, "I assure you that the most winning woman I ever knew was hanged for poisoning three little children for their insurance-money." This is her story.

THE MOST WINNING WOMAN

*I*n the spring of 1895, Holmes and I had just sat down for breakfast when Mrs. Hudson, our faithful housekeeper arrived with a small paper-wrapped box for my friend. After he took it from her and studied the writing on it, the color drained from his lips and his hand shook as he used his kipper knife to slice the string around the box. I rushed to the tantalus and returned with the brandy bottle, adding a drop or two to his morning tea.

From my place behind him, I observed his slow, deliberate moves to unwrap the parcel—as if it might contain some gruesome offering. His cautious efforts called to mind the grisly "present" of two severed ears as recounted in "The Adventure of the Cardboard Box." Fearing what he might uncover, I decided a sip from the brandy bottle might not be out of line for myself as well.

When the contents were finally revealed, however, a wave of disappointment passed through me. The box contained a folded, yellowed document and two other sheets of paper underneath.

He took a sip of his fortified tea and studied first the older document before removing the other two. One, I could discern, was an official death certificate. The second, a letter written in the rather crude and awkward hand of an unedu-cated person.

After reading the letter, he passed all three to me without a word. I took them to my seat, but let my breakfast grow cold while I read them. Holmes also *appeared to have lost his appetite. He merely steepled his hands, his elbows resting on the table, and watched me as I perused the lot.*

The original document was a life insurance policy for a Mr. Jameson Windom. It listed the beneficiary as a Margaret Windom. The death certificate was also for a Jameson Windom, with the cause of death listed as consumption. Finally, I turned my attention to the letter:

> *Dear Mr. Holmes,*
>
> *You are so famus now, you might have foregotin me, but I am keping my promis to you. I am sending you a kopi of my Jameson's deth certifikat to show you I did not kil him and he dyed in his bed of konsumshun. Our dauter Margaret will reseve the insurans moniy.*
>
> *Pleez now reles me from my obligashun.*
>
> *Yours truly,*
>
> *Mrs. Grace Windom*

When I finished, I raised my gaze to meet his, but could tell his thoughts were elsewhere.

"Holmes?" I asked. He started and shook himself as if to settle his thoughts back into the present. "Was she one of your clients?"

His mouth turned down into a grimace. "Hardly. She was.... I'm not sure how to categorize her. An almost-murderess, I suppose, would be the best. Had I not intervened, Mr. Jameson Windom would not have made it to his next birthday. And their daughter Margaret...I suppose she would have been the next victim."

"Good Lord." I drew in my breath. "Why was this packet not sent from a prison? This woman is free?"

"I said she was an almost-murderess. As you can see, her husband died of consumption, and her daughter lives to inherit his insurance. Although I will confirm Margaret thrives. The last time I saw her, she was not yet two. Imagine that. The girl is now a young woman of seventeen or so." He glanced at the ceiling. "Where has the time gone?" Refocusing on me, he asked, "Do you recall I once

told you that the most winning woman I ever met poisoned her children for the insurance money?"

"You mean, Mrs. Windom—?"

He waved his hand, brushing away the words I'd pronounced. "No. No. That woman was Mrs. Josephine Reynolds. A particularly charming woman with as black a heart as ever lived. She hung for her crimes, but I regret not being able to bring her to true justice. Mrs. Windom was another I caught in time."

He finished his tea and pushed his plate back. I had to say, my appetite had disappeared, but my desire to hear the full explanation overwhelmed me.

Following a long moment of contemplation on the scene outside our window, he turned to me. "Given that Jameson Windom is now in his final resting place, I feel I can now share the full details of the package's content." He glanced around the room as his attention returned to the present. "Let's retire to our places by the fire. You may need the warmth, for it is a very cold tale indeed."

Once in our customary places, Holmes stuffed his pipe from the tobacco in his Persian slipper resting on the table beside him. The pipe's smoke drifted toward the ceiling where it curled about on the early-morning breeze coming from the opened window. The room's cheery atmosphere contrasted so with the dark, grim tale he then recounted.

As you know, prior to our arrangements here at 221B, I let rooms on Montague Street and had already done work for Scotland Yard as well as some private clients. My reputation also was growing, thanks to my assistance to Reginald Musgrave, and it was actually through him this case arrived at my doorstep.

Jonathan Barnes arrived with a letter of introduction from Reginald in the fall of 1880. Reginald didn't explain in his missive the exact nature of Barnes' problem. He only noted that Barnes was a tenant on his land, was an honest, hard-working soul, and needed my help.

The man was terribly distraught and could not stand still. Pacing back and forth in front of me, he shared how his brother had passed unexpectedly two weeks ago. "It weren't right, Mr. Holmes, how Malcolm died. The man had barely passed thirty. He was a bricklayer and strong as an ox. A week and a half ago, I gets a telegram from Lila, his wife, saying he died of dysentry. Me poor mum and da were beside themselves. Lord Musgrave—God love 'im—gives us the money to get to London for the burial. But when we arrive, we find Lila's already put 'im in the ground. She sent the telegram two days after poor Malcolm had gone from this earth."

"Dysentery? Had she called a doctor? Did you speak to him?"

"She said she did call a doctor, only's it was too late. Showed me the death certificate he signed. Cause of death: dysentry."

"Do you have the name of this doctor?"

"I copied it from the certificate, but here's the queer part, sir. My brother made enough to keep 'em in house and victuals, but not much more. She was wearin' *new* widow's weeds—not secondhand. I don't know much about those things, but my mum, she's a seamstress, and she said it was the latest style."

"And did you share any of this with the authorities?"

"I tried, sir, but they weren't interested. Said people die of the dystentry all the time. That the water or food can go bad here in the city, and nothin' can save the poor wretch what comes across it."

Something about the earnestness of Mr. Barnes' plea intrigued me. I had to agree with the authorities. Dysentery can be common among the working class. At the same time, the request came from Musgrave, and I felt an obligation to him.

"You have shared some very disturbing turn of events. I will research your brother's death further. Now share with me your particulars, including those of your brother's widow. Once I have more information, I will contact you through Lord Musgrave."

After noting the name and address of the widow Barnes and the doctor's name, he took his leave, and I went to work.

The doctor's surgery was located next to a chemist's shop and near a pub in Whitechapel. His practice barely met the definition of "doctor" or "surgery." The anterior room was filled with the inhabitants of that slum experiencing all kinds of afflictions. His attendant, a woman in a filthy, blood-spattered apron, fairly curtsied when I entered.

"Dr. Kinston is with a patient at the moment," she said, over the screams coming from behind a door, "but I'm sure he'll attend you straightaways, sir."

The doctor had a similar, obsequious manner. "How can I help you, sir? You look fit enough. Got a young lady in trouble? I can fix it."

His offer to perform an illegal act revolted me and instantly marked him as an unscrupulous surgeon. This demeanor made me suspect he was involved in Malcolm Barnes' untimely demise in some fashion.

"I understand you signed the death certificate for Malcolm Barnes. What do you recall of his condition?"

"Barnes?" The short, scruffy man, squeezed his eyes together as if trying to recall. "I sees so many, sir. Do you have an address?" When I provided that bit of information, his face brightened slightly. "Yes. I do recall. A bad case of the dysentery. His wife called me in. Such a pretty, young thing she is. Won't have no trouble finding another husband, that one. I gave him some laudanum for the pain. Next day, his wife come in to tell me he passed in the night and asked for a certificate. Said she needed it for the insurance."

"Do you recall anything odd or different about the man's illness?"

Another puckering of his face and a shake of his head. "No. See a lot of dysentery here. People die of it every day. Course, they have other reasons. Only last week, a woman died givin' birth. Baby boy died too. They brung in a man run over by a wagon in front of my surgery." He shook his head. "Couldn't do nuthin' for him. Expired right there on my table. Happens all the time. You'd be hard-pressed to find a family in this area that ain't lost a loved one or two this past year. Consumption, dysentery, cholera. Sees it all the time. People die here."

While Barnes might have indeed contracted dysentery and passed from natural causes, the doctor's apathetic response to a patient's death raised my suspicions because of two items: the first being that he had not actually viewed the man after he succumbed and that most likely his wife would be the only one with another first-hand knowledge of his last breaths.

Given the doctor's attitude in response to my attire, I changed my dress for that of a laborer's pants, shirt, and cap.

Mrs. Lila Barnes lived not far from the surgery. The woman was not at home, and after some inquiring, I learned she was most likely to be found at a knitting club located a few blocks away. I found it strange that a woman who had so recently lost her husband would attend such a social meeting, and after gaining directions to the club, sought her out there.

The club met in an upper room in a public house called the Wolf and Badger. The pub itself was next to a stable with wagons for hire. I was very pleased when I learned this because there is no better source of information regarding the local population than a publican, and here, the group is right in its midst.

The pub appeared the same as any other in that part of the city with sawdust on the floor that hadn't been changed in years, scarred tables and benches scattered about the room, and the scent of stale beer and gin that burned one's nose. Given the still-early hour, the place wasn't full, but those occupying the bar and tables were a rough lot served by an even-rougher-looking man. Upon entering, I shouldered my way between two men at the bar. No sooner had I ordered a gin than a woman passed through toward a set of stairs at the back. She was dressed in mourning clothes, and when the man returned with my drink, I asked, "Is that Malcolm Barnes' widow? I thought I recognized her."

"No," the man said and wiped the bar in front of me. "That be Amos Hardy's widow. She should be gettin' out of her deep weeds soon. Been gone almost a year now. About half of 'em are in black. I think that's what they do—knit shawls, scarves, and the like for the newly bereaved."

"Surely not all of them are widows?"

"Some have lost a son or daughter, like poor Mrs. Sanders. Both her babies. Or mother or father."

This bit of news immediately struck me. Here was a "club," if you will, for mourners.

"How many women are in the group?"

"I don't count 'em."

"Well, then, how many are up there right now?"

"Twenty, maybe."

"Don't you consider it odd there are so many widows in one place?"

The man had been wiping a glass with a rag, but at my question, he stopped and stared me straight in the eye and responded to me with the same observation as the doctor earlier. "Are you daft? People die here every day."

Despite the assertion by these two men concerning the death rate in this part of London, I couldn't help but feel intrigued by this knitting club for mourners. I turned to follow the woman up the stairs.

The barman, however, put a restraining hand on my arm. "Where do you think you're going?"

"I was hoping to speak to one of the women."

At that point, he squinted at me, scrutinizing me from my head to my toes. I had the feeling that my working man's clothes did not pass muster with him. "They don't like strangers botherin' them, and I don't like it either. I think it best you leave. Now."

The last two words were spoken in a louder voice and appeared to be a signal to others. Several patrons soon surrounded me, and while I was certain my baristu skills would have served me well against any one of them, they outnumbered me at that moment. Knowing discretion is the better part of valor, I took his advice and exited the premises.

Once outside, I considered my next move. I was certain this knitting club required further investigation, but it didn't seem I would easily gain admittance. Not a single man had ascended the stairs.

I was thus pondering alternatives when a woman in plain clothes passed by me and into the tavern, providing me with a plan. While I couldn't gain entrée into this group, I *could* make the acquaintance with a woman who was already a member.

After another hour, the knitting circle appeared to break up, with its members exiting as a group. With most in their weeds, they appeared like a murder of crows flying out of the pub and into the streets in various directions.

The last to leave was the street-dressed woman I'd seen entering earlier. She was a handsome woman, with a fine figure and her hair done up in curls. Her clothes were of a finer quality than those usually found in this district, with a well-turned ankle and a sharp eye. Those widened when I approached her.

"Excuse me, madam, for being so forward," I said and bowed to her. "My name is Neville Adams, and I'm hoping you could help me."

"Mrs. Josephine Reynolds. How could I be of assistance?"

I took a coin from my pocket and held it out to her. "I'm looking for a Mrs. Barnes. Her neighbors said she might be here. I owed him this coin and hoped to pass it to her."

"Yes, poor Lila," she said and clicked her tongue. "She had quite a shock, losing her husband so suddenly."

"I assume now that he's gone, she'll be needing such help. Perhaps you can share her address with me so that I can repay my debt."

She glanced up and down the street, but all the club members had disappeared from the immediate vicinity. "If you like, you can give it to me, and I will pass it on to her."

When she reached for the coin, I pulled my hand back and put it in my pocket. "Excuse me, dear lady, but I prefer to give it to her directly."

"Of course," she said and curled her fingers into her palm before lowering her arm. "You may be glad to know, Mr. Barnes left his wife well provided for. He had a life insurance policy which left her more than one-hundred pounds."

Having already worked several cases with Scotland Yard, I knew one-hundred pounds represented at least a year's wages for someone in Barnes' former line of work, and I expressed my surprise and delight in learning of the man's foresight. "But how do you know of her good fortune? Did she share it with you?"

"Someone else in our little circle told me."

She had a warm way about her. Her large brown eyes widened as she glanced into mine, as if encouraging me to linger longer with hers. After a moment's reflection, I said, "I have neither kith nor kin left here nor else-where. If I were younger, you might call me an orphan. As it is, I am simply alone in this world, and I would be honored if you would join me in a meal."

At this pronouncement, I saw a spark for the merest of seconds—very fleeting—before her eyes softened even more, and she said, "I, too, am alone in this world. I had a husband and three beautiful babies—a happy family. First one, then the other, then the other of our children fell ill. The doctor said it was a stomach fever. They died within days of each other. My poor husband was so distraught, he took to drink and one night, after leaving a pub, fell into the path of a speeding carriage and died as well." After expressing my sympathies, she added, "I think I would very much enjoy accepting your invitation."

When she turned back toward the pub, I hesitated, explaining the publican had taken a disliking to me earlier. She gave a little laugh and said, "You needn't worry. They are suspicious of newcomers, but if you're with me, there'll be no problem. I'm on good terms with him."

With that, I let her pull me in. As predicted, the publican's scowl at my appearance switched to grim acceptance when Josephine smiled and nodded at him. Without a word, he sent two glasses of beer to our table, followed by two bowls of stew, which I had to say was flavorful, although slightly watery and with more onions than I enjoy.

Throughout the meal, she quizzed me about myself, getting my full name and where I was living and working. Her approach was subtle. A less astute man would have not even been aware that he was sharing this information for she was truly a beguiling woman. After we had finished our meal, we lingered over a second beer, and I chose this moment to return to my true interest.

"When I was here earlier, I learned of a group of women who meet upstairs. To knit."

She bobbed her chin. "After I lost my family, I sought some form of solace. A chance to meet with others who had experienced similar heart-break. When I learned of another recently widowed woman, I invited her to my home, and we found knitting a great comfort. It kept our hands busy, but we could also share with each other. Soon, we were inviting more and more women and chose to move into the room upstairs."

"Your group has been successful, from what I can see. I saw several head up the stairs."

"Yes, together we get through and learn to live again by helping each other."

Following the second beer, we left the pub, and I offered to accompany her home, given the hour. She accepted, and soon we were leaving the worst of Whitechapel into a still impoverished, but modest, area. The air didn't carry the stench of decay so prevalent in the other area, and I found her company rather pleasant. Her rooms were above a sundries shop. At the steps, she turned to me and thanked me for the meal.

"My landlady allows me access to the kitchen to prepare my own meals. Let me repay your favor with a home-cooked dinner."

Knowing I still had much to learn about her group, I agreed to come in four days' time. In the meantime, I planned to make my way upstairs to discover any secrets it might hold. Given Josephine's obvious arrangement with the publican, my access would have to be by some subterfuge.

And there was still an examination of any connection Dr. Kinston might have had with Malcolm Barnes' death.

My first move was to rent a room near the pub where I could observe all those entering and leaving. It also served as a place to store my disguises—the first of several I arranged throughout my career. That was where I transformed into Victor, a down-on-his-luck blacking salesman. Each day, Victor would spend his time in a corner of the pub with his sample case, nursing a pint and observing the women's comings and goings to the second floor.

By the middle of the third day, I had determined a pattern, suggesting the knitting club's room would be empty around suppertime when these women would return home to prepare dinner. Because I was to meet Josephine the next day, I decided it was time to discover what lay above.

Such an effort, however, required a diversion to occupy the barman long enough for me to make it up the stairs and inspect the club's rooms. I left the pub early on the third day and watched all the women leave. Returning to the pub in my blacking salesman dress, I burst in with a shout.

"I did, it! I made my quota! Drinks for all!"

I slapped several shillings onto the bar, and the other patrons rushed to be the first to get their free beer or gin. Having completed this step, I waited for the group to finish their first and then their second or third. One group of patrons, who probably had their share and more, became very boisterous, shouting and pushing each other. At that point, I created the distraction needed to slip upstairs. When one from this group rose to make his way to the bar again, I casually extended a foot, causing him to trip and fall into another. The second turned to the first and landed a blow to the man's jaw. The first returned the favor.

Soon, the entire room was filled with men giving and receiving punches. The barman attempted to stop the brawl but was soon the recipient of a few uppercuts of his own. When one particularly fierce jab sent blood spurting from his nose, I took the opportunity to push my way to the stairs and onto the upper floor.

The cries and crashes echoed up the stairs and made the boards underneath my feet vibrate. From the intensity of both, I calculated I had some time to explore this second floor.

And it appeared I would need it, for several doors lined both sides of the hallway. The first two were empty, but the third one I tried was locked. I checked over my shoulder. The commotion downstairs was still going strong, and I had time to pick the latch.

Despite the evening hour, the moon and a corner gaslight provided enough illumination for me to make out a plain room with chairs lining three sides. The fourth side included two cupboards. A table with three bowls stood in its center. What the chamber didn't contain was any evidence of knitting. No bits of yarn covered the floor, no forgotten needles or other knitting items, nothing. As I've noted, the absence of an object can be a clue as much as one present. In this case, clearly these women were not as they professed, and the answer most likely lay in the room's center—the bowls and their content.

Approaching the table, I noted no scent from the bowls, only the sour smell of beer seeping through the floor from the bar below. While the room was too dim to make out the liquid's color, I could tell it was dark but transparent. I dipped my finger into the solution intending to taste it but thought better. Instead, I considered what I might use to carry a bit back with me. How I cursed myself for not having a stoppered bottle with me. From that day forward, I always carried one in my breast pocket for such occasions.

I did, however, have a kerchief in my pocket and soaked some of the liquid in that. A rubbish bin containing some damp papers stood at the far end of the table, and I wrapped the kerchief in them. Thankfully, I had brought my blacking sample case with me and used that to transport the rather sloppy mess.

I now had only to make my way back downstairs without being noticed. Unfortunately, the noise from the brawl had diminished, suggesting the melee's more rowdy instigators had been ejected. I checked the window. I would survive the drop but would most likely be detected when I landed.

As a further complication, I could hear footsteps on the stairs. I surveyed the room in a desperate search for somewhere—anywhere—to hide. Its sparse furnishings offered little concealment. The footsteps grew louder and closer, and I knew that my time was running out. Racing across the room, I opened one cupboard and found it full of boxes. I pulled them out and squeezed into the empty space with only seconds before the door opened.

The voices of two men echoed through the knitting club's room.

An unfamiliar voice said, "See, I told you. There's no one up here."

"There's something wrong, I tells you," said the publican. "Josephine always locks it."

"She just forgot today. You lock it, and let's get back downstairs afores there's another blow-up."

"I don't have it."

The other asked, "What do you mean you don't have it?"

"Josephine didn't give me the key. You're the one watching the place. Didn't she give you one?"

"I'm just a watchman. You're the owner. You don't have a key to your own place?"

"She paid me to let her change the lock."

"Well, come on. There's no one up here. That's all I need to know. I want you to tell her we came up here. Checked everything out."

Their voices were already drifting down the hallway when I finally worked my way out of the cupboard. As I did so, I hit one box, and its content scattered about the floor with a *thud.* I froze, uncertain whether the two men heard the noise, and afraid to move in case they did.

My greatest fears were confirmed when the watchman asked, "What was that?"

"Probably one of the rowdies has come back and lookin' for another row. I best get down there."

"I think it came from Josephine's room. I'm going to check."

"Come with me. I'm going down before my pub's in ruins. I may need your help."

After a moment's hesitation, the watchman said, "All right, but I'm not goin' to take care of Big Tuck this time. The more he drinks, the meaner he gets."

"What are you gripin' about? I helped you earlier."

"But..."

Their voices drifted down the stairs, and I quickly righted the box and gathered the papers that had spilled from it. Other than the bowls on the table, these were the only other items in the room. I tucked a few into my breast pocket for later review, returned the box, and made certain the room was as I had found it.

I still had to find a way downstairs, but the publican had given me an idea. Stepping to the window, I pulled it open and shouted until those lingering about responded, "Free gin at the Wolf and Badger. Hurry before it runs out."

Soon, the noise from those now crowding the pub and demanding their gin rose through the floorboards and echoed down the hallway. As the shouts increased, I let myself out of the room, making certain to lock it behind me.

I crept to the stairwell and peeked down into the pub. A gang of men crowded around the bar, shouting and gesturing at the barman, demanding their gin. He swung a shillelagh back and forth, keeping them from passing over the bar while shouting back that he didn't know what they were talking about. I considered simply slipping out during the melee but felt I owed the barman for having created two disturbances in one hour. When his back was turned away from me, I slapped some coins on the bar and said, "Take care of these men. Gin for all!"

As those already in the pub pushed forward to join those who had come in from the street, I shouldered my way through the crowd and out the door.

After changing in my rooms near the pub, I returned to my quarters on Montague Street to study what I had found in the clubroom.

I analyzed the bowl's liquid first. This turned out to be a rather simple task because now that I could examine the papers from the bin, I found a watermark: "Lady Abigail's Fly Paper." With the studies I had already completed on poisons, I knew this type of fly paper carried not only arsenic but also a bit of sugar, quassia to give it a bitter taste, and brown coloring to make its presence obvious. The papers would be soaked in a saucer of water, to attract and kill flies and other flying pests. Added to someone's tea or coffee, it would be deadly.

The bowls I examined contained no such creatures, and the women would have no need for three bowls of it in one room. To state the obvious, this club was processing poison.

And the papers in my breast pocket provided the reason: insurance money. I'd escaped with three insurance policies: one for Harris Thomas with his wife Amanda listed as the beneficiary and another for Jameson Windom, naming his wife Grace as heir. The third sent a frigid chill down my back, for it listed my persona, Neville Adams as the insured and Josephine Reynolds as the recipient. I recalled our conversation at the pub and all the information she had extracted from me that day. My name, address, and other bits were now part of a policy underwritten by the Essential Insurance Company.

But how did she do it without my signature?

Checking the last page, I found a thumbprint in place of a signature. The two other policies carried similar prints.

With a magnifying glass, I studied each and determined they all belonged to the same person. Only the year before, Sir William Herschel had published his treatise on fingerprints and their use in contracts in India. I had conducted my own research on the subject and came to the same conclusion as Sir Herschel: each person's prints were unique and immutable.

The chill down my spine grew as cold as ice as I contemplated the savagery of this group of women. They were purchasing burial policies for their husbands (and perhaps strangers with no kin like my persona Neville Adams). These were not substantial amounts—about a laborer's annual wage—but more than they would ever see at one time. With the poison they had extracted from the flypaper, they ended the insured's life and collected the benefits. I then recalled a comment Josephine made that took my breath. *"My babies died of a stomach fever."* This group was not content to eliminate their husbands or strangers. Their own children were at risk.

Staring at the policies lying on my table, I contemplated the fate of the other two men. Were the policies in the box that I spilled in the room the next in line to be collected? Tomorrow, I, as Neville Adams, was to dine with Josephine. Was that to be my last meal?

I sprang from my chair, ready to grab my coat and hat, and race to the addresses listed on the documents. I was halfway to the door when I checked my watch. It was half-past one in the morning. If they had been dosed at dinner, it would be too late. I could only hope Amanda Thomas and Grace Windom preferred to administer it in their husband's morning coffee or tea.

And if they *had* ingested the poison?

I needed more of a plan, and a counter-poison would be the first step. My extensive research into poisons included their antidotes as well, and I knew hydrated sesquioxide of iron was recognized as appropriate for arsenic. Just as now, I turned to the chemistry equipment in my rooms and spent the night preparing the compound.

I finished just before dawn and had only enough time to make it to both the Thomas and Windom residences before the men left for work. Because the Thomas residence was slightly closer to my rooms, I stopped there first. My heart dropped to my stomach when I spied a black wreath hanging from the door. I was too late. Death had already visited the house. Hoping the garland was for someone else, I rapped on the door.

Amanda Thomas, already in widow's weeds, answered the door. The woman was a slight woman with a week-old bruise on her left cheek.

"Is Harris here?" I asked in a workingman's accent. "We's gots plans for today."

"Ha-Harris pa-passed away last night," she said, and dabbed a black handkerchief against her eyes.

"Lors, no. What happened?"

She raised her hands to suggest she had no idea. "He had these terrible pains. I called the doctor. He said it was dysentry."

"Oh, that *is* a turrible misery. Me uncle died of it. I'm so sorry. Since I'm here, can I pay me respects?"

I peeked over her shoulder with the goal of possibly getting a glance at Thomas' remains. Her response filled me with even greater dread.

"They already came for-for him," she said with another swipe of her eyes. "The doctor said it weren't safe for him to be in the house with our children. They already were feeling poorly. He said I shouldn't have anyone in."

Her words hit me in the face like a pan of cold water. Not only were these women eliminating family members but selling their bodies to body snatchers. "Resurrectionists," as they preferred to be called, were not above purchasing corpses (no questions asked) for resale to medical schools. I had to stop this fiendish enterprise before the Thomas children suffered the same fate as their father.

I put my hand over my mouth and nose as if I were afraid of the miasma that filled the few rooms. "Harris was a decent chap. I'm sorry for your loss," I mumbled through my fingers and took my leave.

The Windom residence was in an even poorer part of Whitechapel, if that was possible, up two flights of rickety stairs. To my great relief, no wreath adorned this door. A woman with a small girl on her hip answered my knock.

Mrs. Windom was as thin as a broomstick, as if life had already drained her of all vitality. Her blonde hair had been pulled back into a knot at the base of her neck, but most of it had escaped the bun and hung limply down her back. From the doorway, I caught the scents of old food, mold, and despair.

When I asked for her husband, she said, "He's sick. I think it's the desentry. Has dreadful pains. Can't keep nuthin' down."

My heart squeezed in both terror and elation. I was too late for Harris Thomas, but perhaps I would be in time for Jameson Windom. I shoved past her and rushed through the cramped, filthy front room to a dilapidated iron bed covered in a threadbare quilt. The face of the man in the bed was as gray as the pillow on which he lay. I pulled the stoppered antidote bottle from my coat pocket, forced the man's lips open, and poured about half its contents down his throat. He coughed and sputtered, but the compound stayed down. As my panic over the man's fate faded, I found my energy dropping. While Windom wasn't out of the woods, I knew I'd only saved him for the moment unless…

Replacing the stopper with a slightly shaky hand, I spun on my heel and faced Mrs. Windom. She'd followed me into the little bedroom, spouting a barrage of insults and threats. At my sudden movement, she quieted long enough for me to address her.

"Madam—and I use that address loosely—if you don't wish me to call the police immediately for the attempted murder of your husband, you will cease your jabbering."

The glare she gave me in response provided the most animation I'd seen in the woman, but she remained silent.

"Thank you," I said and pointed to the other room. "Now, if you will accompany me to the other room, I wish to have a chat with you. Your answers will determine both your fates."

We sat down in two flimsy chairs at an even more unsteady table. A dirt-smeared glass window let in a thin sliver of light, making the interior even grimmer than when I first entered.

The babe in her arms whimpered slightly, and she bent her head to coo at the child. "This is Margaret," she said. "She's been poorly too." My eyes widened at that remark, but she quickly added, "It's not desentry. She just needs more to eat. I can't—can't…feed her right. If I can't get her more milk…"

Despite her low status, I realized the poor woman still had some compassion—if not for her husband, at least for her child. Perhaps in her mind, one death was justified to save the life of another. I withdrew the policy on her husband from my coat pocket, placed it on the table, and glanced toward the bedroom. "But this is not the answer."

Her eyes rounded at the sight of the policy, then her lips trembled. "I wished I'd never heard of that knitting club or Josephine Reynolds. I knew a woman who lost her husband. She came into a fortune after he died. Said it was from his insurance. She was the one who introduced me to the group."

She went on to describe the scheme I already deduced, but with a few wrinkles I'd never suspected. The "club," if you will, was highly organized and efficiently run through Mrs. Reynolds' oversight. The members pooled their funds to ensure that all were paid on time and would hold a lottery to see whose insured was next. When one woman collected on a death, they split the proceeds according to contributions. As I learned today, they also sold any remains to the body snatchers—unless there were relatives or other family members insisting on a funeral. Their meetings involved a review of the current policies, maintaining all policies up to date, holding lotteries, and extracting the arsenic from the flypaper.

"No one at Essence Insurance ever checks the mark," she said with a shrug when I asked how they could purchase such policies without the person's knowledge. "They are happy to collect our money."

A low groan from the other room, drew me there to check on the latest surviving victim. His eyes were open, but he seemed disoriented. I was able to get him to drink a bit more of the antidote. His wife watched from the doorway.

"What's that you givin' him?" she asked.

"An antidote. Something that counteracts the poison."

"You still goin' to turn me into the coppers?"

I glanced around the room, my gaze resting on the child in her arms and the meager furnishing in the front room. "That all depends. If you'll help me, I'll see about another means of ensuring your future."

"What's I gots to do?" she said with a squint toward me.

"At the moment, I need more information. What's the name of the person who collects and sells the bodies?"

She brightened slightly, as if proud of her knowledge. "That's an easy one. Name's George Tolliver. Has a cousin that has a wagon for hire near the Wolf and Badger. That's how we gets word to him of a death. Hire the cousin's wagon for a delivery at some address."

"Do you know a Lila Barnes?"

She nodded. "Her husband passed less than a month ago. Tolliver picked him up the same day he died. They like 'em fresh as they can."

I took a piece of paper and a fountain pen from my coat pocket and wrote down what she had told me in the form of a confession. It stated she had tried to murder her husband for insurance money by serving him arsenic in his coffee. After reading it to her, I said, "Make your mark and put your thumbprint there."

She pushed back from the table, her eyes growing wide. "You said you'd help me. I ain't signing that. They'll hang me for sure."

"Only if I give it to the authorities. Consider this my own insurance policy to protect your husband—and child. I said I would help you, and I will. But I need assurance that you will not try to harm either in the future. I will keep watch on all of you. If there is ever a suspicious death, I will take this confession to the authorities, and you will have to answer to them and to God." Leveling my gaze to her, I said, "Now make your mark."

She crept back to the table and did as I commanded.

After leaving her with more of the antidote, I put her confession and insurance policy in my coat pocket and stood to take my leave. "Breathe a word of this to anyone, and the confession goes straight to Scotland Yard."

As I stepped out onto the dirty street, I took a deep breath of the fetid air and exhaled slowly. Compared to that in the Windoms' rooms, I felt as if I were breathing in the spring countryside. What I had learned of Josephine Reynolds' scheme and the organization she had created almost rivaled that of another individual of whom I am aware. She had recruited the women in the knitting club, developed a means of selling policies and ensuring their collection, and a process for disposing of the bodies that had operated for some time without raising suspicions.

With Jameson Windom's fate assured for the moment, I turned to my own. After changing into my laborer's clothes and tucking more of the antidote into my coat pocket, I headed to her rooming house. When I reached her street, I kept a vigilant search of all around me. A sense of dread had settled between my shoulder blades as if I carried a target there. Along the way, I contemplated the how her pleasant face and outwardly compassionate personality masked one of the most devious minds I'd ever met. Perhaps it was best that I met such a woman so early in my career, for I took this lesson to hear: one cannot make assumptions by outward appearances, and Josephine Reynolds proved the rule.

As always, she was all smiles and flowers when she answered the door and led me to the small dining table in the kitchen. She'd prepared a curry dish and served us both, along with a beer. I observed her while she labeled the meat and gravy onto two plates. The same with the beer—she served two glasses from the same container. While I couldn't imagine her poisoning herself, I still didn't trust the items weren't contaminated in some form. Pretending to drink the beer and moving my fork in the curry, I gave the appearance of eating without ever ingesting any. I often went without food in the middle of a case, and so, felt no loss—especially when my very life depended on it.

During the meal, Josephine shared about her day in her usual charming manner and even mentioned the death of the husband of one of her knitting club members—to which I expressed my sympathies. All the while, I observed her studying me whenever she thought my attention lay elsewhere. Was she waiting for me to show signs of arsenic poisoning?

When I remained with no symptoms by the end of the meal, she suggested we take a stroll. Once on the street, she linked her arm in mine, and I let her lead us up one street and down another toward the Wolf and Badger.

"Let's have another beer," she said, tugging at my arm to lure me in.

Once seated, two beers arrived at our table. At that moment, I realized the depths of the publican's involvement. The barman's personal attention clearly indicated this beer would, for certain, do me in. I pretended to sip the drink while we chatted. After what I considered an appropriate amount of time, I rose, doubled over, and complained loudly about stomach pains.

"My gut's on fire," I said in a loud voice. I turned to her. "The curry must have been bad."

I lurched forward, knocked over the table with the beers, and shouted, "I'm going to be sick."

The publican and another patron were at my side in an instant. "Let's get you to the street. I'll not be having you soiling my place."

The two grabbed me under the arms and dragged me from the establishment, Josephine following behind me, crying in a distressed voice about my sudden illness.

Once on the street, I had expected them to throw me to the ground and leave me in my misery. Instead, they pulled me up the street toward the corner. Josephine continued close behind, murmuring consolations about my condition and directing them to take me to a doctor.

"I can't stand to see him in such pain," she wailed.

As we reached the corner, a wagon turned from a side street and rattled toward us, and I could feel the men shift their course to lead me directly into its path. I had to react quickly, or I would meet the same fate as Josephine's husband.

I fell to my knees to slow my progress, but it had little effect. The two men continued to drag me to my fate. From my prone position, I could see a crack in one of the horse's hoofs, and the reek of the street's muck filled my nostrils. With only seconds to spare, I pulled my knees under me and pushed upward. The sudden shift of my prone-to-standing position destabilized the other two men. Because he was closer to the street than his companion, the publican fell forward and under the horse's hoofs.

The wagon's driver pulled back on his leads, causing the animal to rear slightly and dislodging its cargo: the remains of Harris Thomas.

The screams from those on the street, the wagon's horse, and other transports passing by called a local officer to the scene. His whistle summoned other nearby police to the street, and arrested all those involved—me, the wagon driver, the barman, Josephine Reynolds, and the good Dr. Kinston. I learned later Josephine had signaled the barman to send for the doctor as soon as we arrived, so that he would be johnny-on-the-spot for signing my death certificate.

While I was still making inroads into Scotland Yard at this stage in my career, I had created a few—among them, Inspector Lestrade. When I laid out the full extent of this woman's organization—the knitting club with the various insurance policies, the production of arsenic, the connection to the resurrectionists, and the help of Dr. Kinston in providing the death certificate—the arrests that followed led to convictions and the execution of Josephine Reynolds and various of her accomplices.

Josephine and seven other women from the club hung for their offenses. Their leader's meticulous records proved to be their undoing. The payments they had made to the various policies and the amount each collected provided the basis for conspiracy charges. Allegations of murder were simply a matter of tracing the bodies (again, thanks to Josephine's records) to the various medical facilities. Additional corpses were exhumed if the deceased was buried. Together, they afforded the evidence needed to substantiate arsenic poisoning. The family of Malcolm Barnes recovered his remains from one of the London hospitals and gave him the proper burial they desired. Interestingly, the amount of arsenic he'd ingested actually preserved the remains, making the return less upsetting —once they clothed the man to hide the students' dissections.

BY THE END of his recounting of the events, the tobacco in his pipe had long since extinguished. Mrs. Hudson had carried away the remains of our breakfast and laid out our lunch, but after this tale, I found I had little appetite.

I shook my head, "To think of the tragic loss of life caused by this woman, and the number of orphans created. Surely the courts showed some mercy to those women with young children?"

"Mercy?" my friend's voice hit a note of incredulity. "What mercy did these women show to any of them? What alternative did the courts have but to take them away from their families? At least the children, orphans though they became, had an opportunity to reach maturity and make something of their lives. Many would have most likely served as additional insurance income to these depraved women. My only regret was that Josephine Reynolds could only be hung once for all the murders she engineered."

Pausing for a moment to consider this observation, I glanced back at the morning mail which had started the retelling of this case, and a thought occurred to me. "And what of Grace Windom? Did you keep your word to her?"

"I wrote to Reginald and explained her role in helping me destroy this murderesses club and solving the disappearance of Malcolm Barnes. For her part, I requested he provide Mr. Windom with some form of employment and to monitor the health of both Barnes and his daughter Margaret. Thankfully, he was very diligent in providing periodic reports on their welfare. You'll be glad to know

Margaret will soon be married to the local blacksmith, and the remittance from her father's insurance (which I will ask Reginald to confirm was of natural causes) should serve nicely for her dowry."

He studied the scene out the window and sighed. "Out of that horrifying tragedy, at least one good did come."

An essential part of a "locked room" mystery is the "summation." In this scene, Holmes will provide others with how the crime was committed. A subpart of the summation is the "summation gathering" where Holmes gathers all the suspects in one room and reveals the culprit.

THE ADVENTURE OF THE MISSING HEIRESS

I stepped off the carriage after my friend Sherlock Holmes and gave a gruff harrumph. "You could have warned me about the mud," I said to his back.

He didn't turn around in answer to my protest, only continued to study the area between our carriage and the estate's entrance. Last night's storm at Baker Street passed through here also. Regrettably, Lestrade and his officers have ruined any potential footprints left overnight."

"How do you know Lestrade made those prints?"

He was still bending over, studying the ground, and spoke over his shoulder. "Because the inspector has flat feet, most likely due to his years of walking London streets. Note the even wear on this print. Flat feet."

We'd been at breakfast when Lestrade's telegram arrived. I'd barely had time to smear some marmalade on my toast before running off after my friend to catch a train to the hamlet of Casterby and the estate of Squire Northridge. With little breakfast and now muddy boots, I was in a rather sour mood. Holmes, however, was already in his brain attic, weaving bits of information together. I studied the surrounding grounds, trying to use the countryside's tranquility to calm me before we delved into whatever crime we'd been called to help resolve.

"The household staff should be admonished," I said, after surveying the area between our carriage and the wall surrounding the estate. "There are horse droppings under that tree."

My friend glanced in the direction I pointed and gave a noncommittal *hmm* before turning to the manor house and a figure passing through the front door. "Here comes the good inspector now. Let's hear his report."

Lestrade strode down the stairs and pulled a notebook from his breast pocket. "So glad you agreed to come, Mr. Holmes. This case will tweak your interest, I'm sure. It's a matter of grave importance. Squire Northridge's daughter, the estate's heiress, is missing. There are no signs of foul play. It's as if she simply vanished."

Sherlock pursed his lips. "I see. And what have you discovered so far?"

Lestrade shifted his weight on his flat feet. "We've done a thorough search of the estate and the surrounding areas. As you can see, despite the rain, we found no foot or wheel prints in the mud. We have also interviewed the staff. The butler and her personal maid were the last to see her. Her maid had locked the windows before leaving her charge last evening. The butler reported having locked all the downstairs windows and doors before going to bed. The other servants retired before the butler."

"But they had visitors earlier in the day," Holmes said.

Lestrade checked his notebook. "How did you—?"

"There are at least three separate piles of horse droppings under the tree over there," he said, pointing to an old oak whose branches reached high and wide near a curve in the carriageway passing in front of the house. "The rain didn't wash them completely away. Only a visitor could tie his horse in front like that."

"You're correct," Lestrade said, consulting the notebook again. "In fact, she had two visitors. Both suitors. The first was a local Baron's son, Humbert Osterling, whose father's estate borders hers. Benedict Whitmore, the son of a prominent Scottish merchant, paid a visit later in the day. The maid and butler suspect Lord Osterling is pushing his son to marry Miss Northridge because he wants to combine the two estates. She met Benedict Whitmore in London at a ball during the season. The maid and butler aren't fond of Whitmore. They think he's beneath her, being the son of a merchant and her the daughter of a squire."

"When did they find her missing?" I asked.

The two turned to me, and I returned their gazes. They appeared a little surprised to see me there, as if they'd forgotten I'd come along.

Lestrade coughed and continued. "Right. Not until this morning. When Miss Northridge didn't request her breakfast at the usual time, her maid checked on her. She had a key and used it to open the locked door. Her bed was never slept in, and the windows were also locked. She alerted the butler, and he checked and found the lower floor's windows and doors remained secured."

"I'd like to examine the grounds and the house, now," said Holmes.

The inspector and I followed behind my friend, giving him the distance he always needed during one of his walkabouts. He first considered the area under Miss Northridge's room, removing a bit of something from a bush underneath the window. He spent some time peering closely at the horse droppings under the tree.

Finally, we accompanied him inside.

"You can see there was no sign of a struggle," Lestrade said. "And her bed was never disturbed."

Once more, my friend responded with a noncommittal sound and inspected the room, examining the bed, wardrobe, floor, and windows.

I had to agree with the inspector. Everything seemed normal to me. Whatever happened to Miss Northridge had occurred before she went to bed, but how could she vanish as she did? Although I anticipated Holmes to search for a secret door or passage by maybe tapping the walls, he instead walked over to her dressing table, which had a few bottles of perfume and a candle. Finally, he stepped to the bed and checked around it, lifting the quilts to glance underneath it.

When he finished, he turned to Lestrade. "I'd like very much to speak to the butler and maid, please."

The two servants waited in the library. A police officer guarded the door. Holmes entered, hands clasped behind his back, deep in thought. The butler sat stoically erect, but his frown spoke of his worry about his charge. The maid wrung her hands in her lap. It was clear she'd been weeping.

My survey of the two suggested both were too distraught to have been involved in the young lady's disappearance. The maid, in particular, elicited my sympathy, and my heart went out to her.

"I do wish I'd not forgotten my pipe. A few puffs would be most enjoyable right now," Holmes whispered to me. He shrugged and studied the two seated figures. "Ah, well. This shouldn't be much longer. I have only a few questions."

Addressing the maid first, he asked, "It's customary for you to help your lady to change into her nightclothes, is it not?"

"Yes, sir," she said with a slight lilt in her voice. "I helped her into her nightgown and put a dressing gown over it, as I always do."

"Did you turn down the bed?"

"Yes, sir. But she never slept in it."

Turning to the butler, he asked, "And you heard nothing odd last night?"

"No, sir. Only the storm."

He spun about and gave a hard stare at the maid. "Where," he asked in a demanding voice, "has Miss Northridge gone with Whitmore?"

My eyes widened involuntarily, and both Lestrade and I stared at the older woman. She blinked back tears, but the white of her cheeks belied her guilt.

No evidence needed, Lestrade turned to the officer by the door. "Arrest her for the kidnapping of Miss Northridge."

With a shriek, the poor maid buried her face in her hands. "I didn't do anything to my lady. I love her like my own daughter. Please don't arrest me."

Holmes held up a hand to stay the officer. "Did I ever say she kidnapped her? I merely asked where she was. She has knowledge I need her to share."

"I'll tell you anything," she said with a wail. "Just don't send me to jail. I only did what she asked me. They've gone off to Gretna Green to marry."

My heart jerked. Elopement. Had she eloped with the Scottish merchant's son, the required waiting period for the marriage would be unnecessary. His residency eliminated the 21-day wait required for those who are not Scottish. They would most certainly complete the ceremony before anyone could catch them.

"Tell us everything," Lestrade said in his most demanding voice.

"The baron and his son was puttin' a lot of pressure on my lady. Sayin' if she didn't marry his son, he'd arrange for Whitmore to be arrested. He'd set up a case against him. Whitmore is the love of her life, and she, his. You should see them together, sir. Never seen a truer pair of love birds than them two."

"And last night, you helped her escape through her window," Holmes said, prompting her to continue the story. "She used the sheet from her bed. One missing, and I found a small piece of it caught in the bush underneath the window. I must say you did an excellent job of creating the illusion that both sheets were still there."

"That's right. I merely folded over the bottom sheet to make it appear as two."

"Whitmore was waiting for her under the tree. I found three piles of horse droppings, two much more affected by the rain than the third. The last one had not been there as long. They waited for the rain to wash away any hoofprints."

"Yes, sir. It'd been days without rain. She was fairly giddy when we heard the wind pick up."

"She signaled Whitmore from the window with a candle. I found wax drippings on the casement of one."

"Yes, sir. It was already comin' down somethin' fierce, but the brave girl she is shimmied down the sheet despite it all."

"But you didn't let her go empty-handed. She took a small valise with her nightclothes, the dressing set from her table, and a few gowns. These were all missing from her room."

Her face shifted into the hard lines of a frown. "I knew I should have taken the hangers from the wardrobe."

"Not your only mistake, my dear," Holmes said. "You failed to replace the brush and mirror from the table. No woman has only perfume for grooming. But I must compliment you on your clever efforts to hide her escape."

"Oh, it weren't me," said the maid, her eyes crinkling slightly. "It were my lady. She's quite a clever one all on her own. She come up with the plan. I only helped her."

Holmes gave a nod of acknowledgment. "I see. Well, thank you for your cooperation. You may go now, but I suggest you leave the estate until the baron comes to accept the marriage."

"Oh, yes, sir. I'll be goin' to Scotland as soon as I can to be with my lady."

"I fear the baron won't easily let this affair go," I said, worried for the young lovers. "He might go through with his threat to have Whitmore arrested."

"I think Miss Northridge—or such I say Mrs. Whitmore?—will be thrilled with her new life in Dundee. And Whitmore himself is well situated to battle any accusations Lord Osterling throws his way. Not when he's the heir to a marmalade fortune."

Echoing Lestrade's earlier question, I asked, "How did you know—?"

"Elementary," said Holmes. "Did you not read the label on the marmalade jar this morning? You spread Whitmore Marmalade, made in Dundee, on your toast. Once again, you saw, but didn't truly observe."

THE ADVENTURE OF LAFITTE'S MISSING TREASURE

It was one of those languid Saturday afternoons in the fall of 1894 when the package arrived. By this time, Holmes had once more established himself in his Scotland Yard consulting practice after his years abroad when everyone—including myself—thought he had fallen to his death at the Reichenbach Falls, and we had both returned to our routines at 221B.

Between the day's temperate climate and Mrs. Hudson's plentiful breakfast, I wanted to curl up in my customary chair and doze like one of those cats some ladies fancy. My eyelids seemed peculiarly heavy, and I might have allowed them to close had it not been for Holmes' pacing. Having solved some interesting cases, which I had yet to put to paper, such as that of the missing heiress and the adventure of the leopard's spots, he now complained no new adventure had crossed his path to task his mind. I feared if no such case appeared, he might be tempted to return to his old cocaine habit—after I had weaned him off that terrible addiction.

The package's arrival, then, was a blessing for us both. It pulled me from my near-catatonia and Holmes from his inner ruminations.

After thanking our dear housekeeper for the delivery, my friend examined the packet carefully before taking it to his desk to open.

I joined him at the other side of the desk for a better view of what it held inside.

"It's traveled a long way," I said, observing the address. "New Orleans, Louisiana."

An absent-minded *mm-hmm* was his only response as he slid a penknife along one side of the packet. Tipping the opening toward the desk, he let its contents spill out. A heavy gold coin fell with a muted *thump* onto a pile of newspapers awaiting Holmes' review.

Two sheets of folded paper floated after.

Holmes retrieved a magnifying glass from the desk drawer to study the coin more closely while I unfolded one paper, leaving the other for later review.

Immediately upon opening the missive, I said, "It's from a woman."

"I could have told you that from the handwriting on the packet," he said as he stepped to the window to better study the coin in the sunlight. "Would you care to read it aloud?"

"Dear Mr. Holmes," it began. "I come to you with a matter of utmost urgency. My husband, Mr. George West, has disappeared, and I fear for his safety. He was last seen aboard the ship 'The Southern Empress,' which was sailing to Galveston from New Orleans. No one has heard from him or any of the crew for over a week."

I glanced up from the paper. "Galveston, Texas. Where is that, exactly?"

Holmes paused to turn the coin over and continued his examination. Without raising his gaze, he said, "On the southern coast of the United States, Watson. Known historically for its hurricanes, pirates, and, unfortunately, yellow fever outbreaks."

"Doesn't sound like a very inviting place," I mumbled mostly to myself.

"I wouldn't say that. It's currently considered 'The Wall Street of the Southwest.' And I may have yet another example of that wealth here."

"You mean that coin?"

"In a manner of speaking. Please continue the letter."

"My husband has always considered himself something of a historian but has limited himself to treasure hunting. He has become obsessed with the pirate Jean Lafitte, a privateer who operated first out of New Orleans and later, Galveston. Talk of Lafitte's missing treasure has been a matter of speculation for more than seventy years. The pirate established a base on Galveston Island in 1817 but was forced to leave in 1820 after attacking an American merchant vessel.

"Recently, a Mr. James Farthington approached my husband, stating he had found a letter written to one of Lafitte's acquaintances detailing the location of a treasure buried on the island. As proof, Lafitte included this coin for the friend. My husband agreed to finance the search in return for half the find.

"A week ago, George and Farthington set off for the island. There have been no storms or other occurrences that would explain his ship's disappearance, and I, therefore, fear the worst. Someone has heard of this discovery, and the expedition has fallen into nefarious hands and my husband is in grave peril.

"Given the distance, by the time you get this letter, another week will likely have passed. Please respond by telegram as soon as possible to let me know if you have any advice on how I might find George and the others."

When I turned to the other piece of paper, I found the thin paper held a map. "It looks as if she included a copy of the directions Farthington shared with her husband."

Holmes lowered the coin and returned to the desk, where he held out his hand. I placed the map into it, and he held it up to the light. "A very lightweight paper used for tracing. She must have traced the original map to share a copy with me." He faced me. "It seems we have a mystery on our hands, Watson. And one that may lead us to uncover the lost treasure of Jean Lafitte."

My interest was piqued. "Lost treasure? Sounds like something from a yellowback novel."

Holmes waved a hand dismissively. "It is not a fairy tale, Watson. Jean Lafitte was a real pirate, and there have always been rumors of a treasure buried somewhere on Galveston Island. Many have searched for it over the years, but none have discovered its whereabouts."

"So, you believe that this Farthington fellow may have discovered the location of the treasure, and now someone is after it and them?"

"It is a possibility, Watson. And one that we cannot ignore."

"Then what do we do?"

"Send off some telegrams."

For the next half hour, Holmes prepared three telegrams and sent our page Billy to the telegraph office. After that, he changed from his smoking jacket into a hat and coat.

"Would you like me to accompany you?" I asked as he headed toward the door.

Turning back to me, he shook his head. "I appreciate the offer, my friend, but I'm going to consult a coin expert who is rather eccentric and something of a recluse. It is doubtful he would receive both of us. I shouldn't be more than an hour or so. In the meantime, please be so kind as to wait for any responses to my telegrams."

While I felt he had given the assignment more out of pity than any great concern for the arrival of a few telegrams, I consented to remain behind.

After Holmes left, I settled back into my chair and pondered the case at hand. It was certainly intriguing, and the possibility of discovering lost treasure stirred my imagination and prompted me to do some research of my own. Turning to Holmes' extensive library of encyclopedias and notebooks full of clippings on any variety of subjects, I found accounts of Lafitte's exploits as a privateer as well as mentions of his treasure—but nothing specific concerning its location.

While the man had once run a very successful smuggling operation in New Orleans and other ports in Louisiana, he was forced out in 1817. He moved his operations to the island of Galveston. There, he and his men founded a town that grew to 2000 inhabitants and 120 structures. The grandest was, of course, his own *Maison Rouge*. This red house actually had a moat around it. After only four years, Lafitte left the island, forced out by the US Navy after one of his captains attacked an American merchant ship.

Given the urgency with which he had to leave the island, it was rumored he buried some of his treasure there with the plan to return for it. But before he left, the *Maison Rouge* and other structures were burned, making it more difficult to find the exact location of the buried treasure.

The daringness of this "gentleman pirate" and his amassed fortunes intrigued me. Robert Louis Stephenson's tales of pirates and buried treasure paled in some comparisons to actual fact. I found myself understanding George West's fascination, imagining myself standing on the deck of a ship, prepared to capture and board another vessel to take for myself the gold and other valuables in its hold.

So deep was I in thoughts and flights of fancy that when someone knocked on our door, I searched for my cutlass, ready to battle the invader. By the time I rose to my feet, I was back at 221B and thanking Mrs. Hudson for bringing me two telegrams that had arrived together. She had carried them up on a tray holding my afternoon tea.

I selected one and saw it was from the Port of New Orleans:

"Ship records show that 'The Southern Empress' set sail from New Orleans with Mr. West and Mr. Farthington aboard. No distress signals were received. Will update if any new information comes to light."

My hands trembled slightly with a mixture of elation and dread as I re-read the message. The telegram confirmed the existence of Farthington, West, and the ship, but also no sign of the ship facing any disasters. It also provided no information on the ship's whereabouts or destination.

The second telegram, from the local constabulary, confirmed that a Mr. and Mrs. George West did reside at the address Mrs. West had supplied in the original packet. Furthermore, Mrs. West had visited the station to report her husband missing two days before she wrote to Holmes.

I set the telegrams next to Mrs. West's original envelope on Holmes' desk and planned to return to my chair for further research on this pirate when footsteps echoed through the hallway. After hearing the same tread over these many years of friendship, I knew my friend had returned.

When he entered, I asked, "Was your numismatist able to shed any light on the coin?"

Holmes removed his hat and coat and hung them by the door. He then helped himself to a cup of tea. "Yes, he confirmed that the coin is indeed from the early 1800s and is consistent with the period in which Lafitte was active. He also believes it to be from a private mint, which would have been consistent with the practices of the time."

I leaned forward, eager for more information. "And did he have any insights to help interpret the map?"

"He did not, but he did make a rather unusual suggestion." He paused and glanced out the window. "I hadn't realized it was getting so late." He set down the teacup with a clatter and strode quickly to his room. Over his shoulder, he said, "I'll be going out again, Watson. Don't wait up for me."

About twenty minutes later, a weathered seaman entered our living room. Had I not known Holmes' ability for disguise and that only he could have entered the room from his bedroom, I would have never recognized my friend as this sun-browned, wind-burned old sailor.

"I'm off to the docks in search of someone who knows the waters between Galveston and New Orleans. With any luck, both the whereabouts of Mr. West and the treasure can be deduced."

WHEN I ENTERED the room for breakfast the next morning, a scruffy old sailor sat in my place, helping himself to my coffee and scones. His shaggy hair and beard were more gray than black, his boots were of weathered leather, and his canvas shirt was open to reveal a clipper ship sailing across his chest. Despite the open window allowing the early morning breeze to enter, the room carried the scents of musty wool, salt, and raw fish.

"Good morning," I said.

The man stopped slurping his coffee long enough to grunt at me before continuing to slather half a pot of jam on the last of the scones. My stomach growled at the sight of the bread sliding into his mostly toothless mouth. I could only hope Mrs. Hudson had additional pastries in her kitchen.

With a step backward toward the middle of the room, I called out over my shoulder to my friend. "Holmes?"

"Ah, Watson, I'm so glad you're here," he said when he exited his bedroom. While he still wore his sailor clothes, he had removed the makeup from his face. "Allow me to introduce Monsieur Francois

Moreau, a former sailmaker's assistant. He served on several crews in the Gulf of Mexico and is quite familiar with the coastline."

"*Oui*," he said in a hoarse voice and returned to emptying the coffee pot into his cup.

"He agreed to return with me to study the map Mrs. West provided. His keen memory and knowledge of both the New Orleans and Galveston coastlines have provided an excellent understanding of the positions shown on the map."

I nodded, taking a seat opposite the sailor in Holmes' usual place and helped myself to a cup of tea—the coffee having been depleted. "And have you solved it?"

"It seems that the map Mrs. West provided us with is not a map of the region as it currently exists. In fact, it appears to have been drawn from memory by someone who knew the area well but did not have access to modern cartographic tools."

Holmes poured himself a cup of tea and moved to his desk where the coin and papers lay.

"*Oui*," Moreau said with a grunt and picked at the crumbs caught in his beard. He chewed for a moment, then said, "*La Maison Rouge*."

I perked up, pleased to contribute to the conversation. "I read about it. That was Lafitte's home in Galveston."

Moreau shoved himself back from the table and marched to the desk. He stabbed a stubby forefinger onto the paper. "*La Maison Rouge*." He moved his finger about an inch to the right of the original spot and raised his gaze to me. His beard parted to form a smile reflecting greed and triumph. "The treasure."

"Do you truly think West is there?"

"If he survived the trip. According to Monsieur Moreau, the areas at the end of the islands have very strong currents in which a man could drown. There are also sandbars that can appear at low tide and run a ship aground."

"The sea can be *dangereuse*," the Frenchman said with a knowing nod. He truly was a man of few words.

I considered the information shared so far, and asked, "What do you propose next? Going to Galveston?"

"Not a very logical move. The trip would require too many days at sea. I have another plan in mind. With Monsieur Moreau's knowledge of the area, I have been able to construct a more accurate map and have pinpointed the treasure's location on what Mrs. West sent to us."

He pulled a drawing from under Mrs. West's letter and spread it flat. Retrieving a compass from a desk drawer, he drew a circle around the X marked on the new map. "I surmise they buried the treasure within an area of about ten feet from this point. I have already calculated the longitude and latitude of this point and plan to pass the information on to Mrs. West."

"Brilliant, Holmes," I said, beaming, and turned to the old seaman. "And I'm certain that Monsieur Moreau deserves a 'job well done' as well. It is early, but given you have not yet gone to bed, I think a drop of brandy or two in celebration is in order."

I went to the sideboard and filled three snifters from the bottle in the tantalus. Moreau's tongue traveled around his lips in anticipation. He fairly grabbed the glass from my hand and downed it in one gulp.

Holmes took his glass but set it aside before tasting it. Instead, he took several blank pieces of paper from the desk drawer and composed another series of telegrams. Turning to Moreau, he handed him a coin and the papers. "Thank you very much, Monsieur Moreau. Your services have been most helpful. Please be so kind as to pass these to Mrs. Hudson for Billy to take to the telegraph office on your way out."

Moreau nodded and tucked the coin and papers into his pocket before lumbering out of the room, casting a longing glance at the brandy bottle on the sideboard as he went.

Once we were alone, I turned to Holmes. "Do you think it wise to pass the location to Moreau? I don't think a single one of those telegrams will arrive at their destination."

"I don't anticipate that they will. I have a new set of telegrams to send off."

With that, he spent the next quarter hour preparing three telegrams. After confirming with Mrs. Hudson that Monsieur Moreau had never passed her way when he left, he handed her the new batch, requesting she arrange their delivery. When she left, I studied my friend carefully. While his face was unreadable, I could sense excitement building within him. He stepped out of the apartment once again, but this time with a spring in his step that signaled he was on the verge of a major breakthrough. I found his enthusiasm contagious, putting me in a restless mood as well. I waited on pins and needles to witness the conclusion of what he had set in motion.

Unable to concentrate, I alerted to every sound on the street or creak in the house. Even Mrs. Hudson had been infected. She was forced to make three trips up the stairs with our dinner because she kept forgetting items. Of course, her efforts were in vain when it came to Holmes. He was in such a state, he only helped himself to a cup of tea. I, too, only picked at the repast, a victim of both my own nerves as well as our landlady's. The meal wasn't one of her best attempts.

After several hours of such agitation, I decided to retire to my bedroom (although I doubted sleep would come easily). To my delight and dread, a knock at the outside door made both of us jump. Moments later, Mrs. Hudson's quick step on the stairs told us whatever had been announced below carried some urgency.

She stood in the doorway, her hand on her chest as if to slow her heart or her breathing—or possibly both. "Mr. Holmes, you have received *three* telegrams."

"Thank you," he replied, taking them from her. "Please have Billy at the ready to carry any response to the telegraph office."

She nodded but remained where she was.

"Something else?" he asked her.

With a glance first at the floor, she shifted slightly on her feet and said, "I was hoping to hear the replies."

I could feel my lips twitching slightly. The woman was as curious as I, and who could blame her? The entire case resembled a play read in the dark. All the events occurred an ocean away, and our only insight into the action was passed through a series of brief reports.

After studying the envelopes of each telegram, he opened one, read it, and passed it to me.

"It's from the New Orleans constabulary," I said and read it aloud for Mrs. Hudson's benefit as well. "In response to your suggestion, we questioned the staff at the West residence. They reported Mrs. West left to visit relatives three days after her husband. The servants were to forward any correspondence to an address in Galveston."

As I considered the implications of this news, Mrs. Hudson drew in her breath. "Oh, that wicked, wicked woman."

"You mean, her husband—?" I didn't complete the sentence with the realization that Mrs. Hudson had understood the implications before I had.

"Yes. It was as I feared when I received no response to my earlier telegram. I believe she and Farthington have some sort of previous liaison. While Farthington distracted West on their trip, she contacted me hoping I could identify the treasure's location using my own investigative skills," he said with a frown.

"And her husband has most likely met some terrible fate," I said, understanding the implications of Holmes' deductions.

"Precisely," he said and handed me another telegram. "Read this from the US Lifesaving Service in Port Aransas, Texas."

"Dear Sir, thank you for your advice on a possible shipwreck near the coast of Galveston. Found the ship Southern Empress grounded on a sandbar. All but two were rescued. Mr. George West and Mr. James Farthington are feared missing after they left in a dinghy to seek help."

"Good lord," I said. "What about the treasure? Will Moreau beat the others to it?"

Handing me the final telegram, he said, "I think the Texas Rangers have everything well in hand."

The third telegram read, "Your reputation has traveled here to Texas, Mr. Holmes, and we are indebted to you for your swift warning regarding the Lafitte treasure and related murder. When we arrived at the location you provided, we came upon what could only be described as a battlefield. A group of what appeared to be sailors had exchanged shots with a group of laborers, presumably hired by Farthington and Mrs. West—both now deceased. We arrested all survivors until we determine their contributions to the mayhem and any clues to the whereabouts of Mr. George West. The treasure itself remains to be uncovered. The Rangers will be excavating the area to discover and claim the treasure in the name of the great state of Texas."

"Mr. Holmes," our landlady said, drawing in an excited breath, "you solved a case thousands of miles from here without even leaving the city."

"Four thousand, eight hundred and forty-seven miles, to be exact," he said and sighed. "Now, if you don't mind, I think I shall retire for the evening. I've been up for a while now."

With that announcement, he left us, closing his bedroom door firmly behind him.

The case's last stroke came a week later when a box arrived with the afternoon mail. Holmes had gone out on another case, reducing Mrs. Hudson and me to bundles of nerves while we awaited his return. It took all my willpower not to attack the strings securing its contents, and I almost assaulted my friend when he finally returned home.

"Holmes, if you do not open this box immediately, I will truly lose all my self-control and open it myself," I said, having lost all composure.

He chuckled as he finally opened the box. "There, Watson, satisfy your curiosity."

Inside the box, I removed first a very impressive parchment, a letter, and a gold coin.

Deciding to start with the letter, I opened and noted the heading. "It's from the governor of Texas. 'Dear Mr. Holmes, the state of Texas wishes to express its gratitude for your assistance in capturing a murderer and solving one of the great mysteries of our state—the existence of the lost treasure of Jean Lafitte. We will be eternally in your debt for restoring to the state treasury these valuable artifacts from our colorful history. As a reward, please find the enclosed coin from the buried chest found by our diligent Texas Rangers only a few feet from the location you pinpointed for them. It is also my great pleasure to declare you an honorary citizen of Texas, with all the rights and privileges afforded thereto, as the certificate indicates. Please know if you should ever choose to visit our state, our Congress is prepared to honor you with a 'Sherlock Holmes' Day.' Sincerely, etc."

Holmes studied the parchment, coin, and letter when I handed them to him. "I suppose these will be some interesting additions to your dispatch box at Cox and Company."

"You aren't going to display them? That coin must be worth—"

"It's blood money, Watson. Not only did several die in this incident, much of Lafitte's wealth originated from the sale of slaves. That does not even consider the lives lost when he attacked and captured the ships. This 'gentleman pirate' was no gentleman. The only satisfaction I take in this case is that the treasure, now found, will not lure others into the same trap."

In seven of the original Sherlock Holmes cases, he is called upon to find a missing person, including a bride on her wedding day, a student, a rugby player, and an independent woman. One of these original stories "The Disappearance of Lady Frances Carfax" appears later in this book. But in the following case, the missing person is a little different.

THE DISAPPEARANCE OF LORD BOATSWAIN

J had arrived back to 221B after a morning at my surgery only to find Holmes putting on his coat and hat in preparation for leaving the flat.

"Watson, you've come just in time. No, don't take off your hat. My brother Mycroft has requested I meet Inspector Lestrade at the Earl of Mayweather's manor house. Apparently, Lord Boatswain has disappeared, and he has asked for my assistance in the matter."

With a sigh, I followed him back down the stairs to the street where we hailed a hansom to take us to the train station. I'd been looking forward to some quiet time after a day on my feet, treating a series of complaints from my patients.

It wasn't until we had settled into the cab's seat that something occurred to me. "I don't believe I'm familiar with Lord Boatswain."

My friend frowned. "Now that you mention it, I don't believe I have either. I didn't have time to research the gentleman in my files. Mycroft's note read 'Urgent.' He sent an undersecretary to run it over personally."

The earl's residence was a grand and sprawling manor with tall windows in its ornate facade overlooking lush, landscaped gardens. A stiff butler met us at the door and ushered us into a morning room where

Lestrade and an elegantly dressed man I assumed to be Lord Mayweather were seated, apparently awaiting our arrival.

The briefest of introductions were made, and Holmes initiated his investigation by asking the earl, "When did you last see Lord Boatswain?"

"My wife checked on him just before she retired for the evening. His room is next to hers."

Holmes, his hands clasped behind his back, had been studying the carpet during the answer. He raised his gaze and asked, "Can I assume that Lord Boatswain is a brown short-haired dachshund? And that while he is not the most mannered dog, you are quite fond of him?"

Mayweather's eyes rounded slightly. "How did you—?"

My surprise equaled his but for different reasons. I'd thought we were investigating a missing person. Not a missing dog. What had possessed Mycroft to call Holmes in on such a case? Holmes, however, seemed to have some understanding of the significance of the canine's disappearance. Without mentioning any earlier misunderstanding of the victim's pedigree, he focused instead on his conclusions regarding Boatswain's identity.

"There are short, brown hairs on some of their chair cushions and teeth marks on some of the furniture's legs. The marks, however, are all near the floor, suggesting a short animal. That you tolerate the animal to do such damage and allow it to sit on the chairs indicates you have great affection for the dog."

"I'm afraid my wife does indulge him more than most would. He is, of course, a prize-winning animal, but more importantly, he gives her great pleasure. I tolerate him because she adores him so. We were not blessed with children, and she has placed all her motherly attentions on him and his predecessors. His disappearance has upset her so, she is unable to rise from her bed. He was supposed to compete in a show in London next week, and I fear he was taken to keep him from competing."

"Your brother called you in because of concern for Lord and Lady Mayweather's safety," Lestrade said, finally breaking his silence. "If someone is able to kidnap Boatswain from his room right next to the Countess, the security of all may be compromised."

Holmes and I both nodded. I might not have Holmes' powers of deduction, but I did know Lord Mayweather was involved in matters of trade and negotiations of trade agreements with different countries. If Mycroft considered the missing canine important enough to summon his brother, national security must be involved, for this was at the heart of Mycroft's duties. His keen understanding and sense of threats to the British Empire were central to our continued power and prosperity.

After pondering the current situation, Holmes brow furrowed into even deeper lines. "No one has heard from the kid—er, dog—nappers?" he asked. When he received a negative reply, he shook his head. "Odd. Very odd indeed."

Glancing around the room, he spun on his heel and took long strides toward the door. Speaking over his shoulders, he said, "I assume Boatswain's room is upstairs? Which is it?"

The three of us scrambled to keep up with him as he bounded up the stairs. The earl called up after him, "The second door on the right. Please, don't disturb Lady Mayweather."

The three of us caught up to him just after he entered the room. He held up a hand to keep us from entering. We stood in the doorway, all huffing slightly from our rapid ascent. Holmes was already deep into his investigative stance. Hands clasped behind his back, he stood silently in the room's center and slowly turned as he considered each and every item in the room.

I have to say that Lord Boatswain lived better than I. His room was at least three times the size of my modest bedroom at 221B. A small, short replica of a four-poster bed replaced a human-sized one on the left side. An oriental carpet, so soft my feet sank into its pile, reached almost to the room's four corners. China bowls near the windows held some food and water. A wardrobe stood on the right. Toys filled a chest next to the bowls.

Holmes first examined the carpet, getting on his knees and peering across it in all directions. "When was this room last cleaned?" he asked.

Mayweather responded immediately. "The maids come about midday when Lord Boatswain is taken for his walk. A footman came in this morning to take him outside. That's when we discovered he was missing."

My friend turned to the bed. Even from my position, I could see it had been disturbed. After examining it with a magnifying glass he pulled from his coat pocket, he turned to the wardrobe. The door had been slightly open, and he now pulled the door back completely and asked the earl, "Do you notice anything missing?"

"His plaid coat," he said. "He would have worn it this morning because of the chill. Maybe the footman got it out before he saw Boatswain was missing?"

"Would he have taken a leash as well?"

The man pointed to a series of hooks on the wardrobe door. Three hung there, but the third was empty. "You're right. There *is* one missing."

Holmes took out each leash, holding it at arm's length and then replaced it to examine the next.

"We must speak with the footman immediately."

"He's most likely in the kitchen with the other servants," he said. "Follow me."

We returned downstairs, Mayweather leading the way to a formal dining hall, then down a flight of steps at the back of the room. Muted conversations and the scent of cooking vegetables and meat drifted up the stairwell as we descended.

The majority of the servants were seated at a long wooden table, a cup of tea or some piece of work in front of each. When the earl entered the room, a cacophony of scrapping chairs followed when they all stood to greet their employer. His gaze settled on one rather nervous-looking young man in livery at the far end of the table with downcast eyes.

"Willoughby, this gentleman has a few questions to ask you."

"I think I'll take over now," Lestrade said and pulled a pair of darbies out of his coat pocket. "Willoughby, you're under arrest for the kidnapping of Lord Boatswain."

The young footman's cheeks paled, his eyes rounded and his chin trembled. I feared he might faint dead away—and me without my smelling salts.

Before he could sputter out little more than, "But-but-but...," Holmes came to his defense. "Really? What makes you think this man had anything to do with his disappearance?"

"Because he was the one who reported the loss." Lestrade gave my friend a glare that would have brought a less controlled man to fisticuffs. "We all know that the one who cries 'thief' the loudest is the thief."

"I don't think he shouted anything," Holmes said. He focused on Willoughby and asked, "Please account for your time in the last twenty-four hours."

"Me, sir?" The color was returning to his cheeks, and he took a deep breath before responding. "Yesterday, Lady Mayweather sent me to town to fetch some bones from the butcher. Cook had served chicken, and it ain't safe to give them to a dog. I come back and brought them to Lord Boatswain's room. He were there with Lady Mayweather and Bristol—"

"Who is this Bristol?" Holmes asked.

The earl coughed and said, "He is Lord Boatswain's personal assistant. Or should I say 'was.' My wife dismissed him yesterday. She claimed he was abusing him."

At this news, I could not contain myself, being rather fond of the canine species. "Good lord. Of course, he was dismissed. He should be dealt the same blows he gave the animal."

"It weren't like that," said a young woman in a cook's apron and cap. "Mr. Bristol is quite fond of Lord Boatswain." Her eyes filled with tears. "It were all my fault, but Milady wouldn't let him explain."

"We are now," said my friend. "Please continue after you provide us your name."

By now, tears were sliding down her cheeks, but her voice was steady enough. "I'm Annie, Cook's assistant. As Willoughby said, we had prepared chicken curry for the meal yesterday. After we took the meat to put in the sauce, I thought the barn cats might like to have the bones."

"But it's as dangerous for cats to eat the bones as a dog," I said, unable to restrain myself. I'm not as fond of cats as dogs, but as a physician, I've been called upon more than once to tend to a cat with a bone lodged in its throat. No animal should suffer that fate.

She turned her gaze to meet mine, and a lump caught in my throat. I could read the remorse in her features. Whatever she'd done, she truly regretted it. I feared her next words might send Lestrade to switch the darbies to her. I wasn't sure I could stand to see this young lady—more of a girl really—shackled.

New tears welled in her eyes. "I know that now, sir. I'd taken the bones to the cats in the barn, and one started choking almost immediately. I didn't know what to do, so's I ran to fetch Mr. Bristol. He knows about dogs, so I thought he might knows about about cats, too."

"And did he?" Holmes asked, returning to his role as grand inquisitor.

At this, the girl brightened slightly. "Oh, yes, sir. He was ever so clever about picking out the bone in Charlie's—that's the cat's name—gullet. But —" Her face clouded again, and she glanced at Lord Mayweather. "He put the bones in his pocket to keep the cats from eatin' any more. I suppose he forgot he had 'em when he went back to Lord Boatswain's room."

"And that's how Lord Boatswain came to eat a chicken bone, and why Lady Mayweather dismissed his personal assistant," Holmes said with a conclusive air. "I most certainly need to speak to Mr. Bristol.

He hesitated before speaking in a rather guilty tone. "I'm afraid I can't help you there, Mr. Holmes. When Lady Mayweather dismissed him yesterday, she saw that he was escorted from the estate. I have no idea where he went."

Holmes studied each of the servants who had been observing this discussion, but I noticed nothing but blank stares in response. If someone knew where Bristol had gone, they were hiding it well.

Holmes sighed, perhaps as disturbed about this turn of events as I. "No one knows where Mr. Bristol might be?" They all shook their heads—almost in unison.

"Seems rather suspicious to me," said Lestrade. "I'll send a report to Scotland Yard to be on the lookout for this character, possibly with a dog. I'll need a description."

His gaze fell on the earl. He shifted his weight and said, "Certainly. He is tall, broad-shouldered, with a very strong jaw. Brown hair and blue eyes."

Lestrade jotted this all down and noted he would be sending a telegram straight away. While the inspector had been speaking Holmes had been studying Annie. I noticed the girl's eyes were downcast, but I took that as more of her remorse for her part in the chicken bone incident.

Lestrade headed toward the door, but Holmes called out to him before he'd taken only a few steps. "Before you contact the Yard, I need to visit the stables. If you'll be so kind as to stay with the staff while Lord Mayweather escorts us to the barn."

Lestrade's mouth pulled down. While he said nothing, I was certain he wanted to get the man's description to headquarters as soon as possible. The delay disturbed me as well, but I knew better than to argue with my esteemed companion when he was on the hunt.

We all trooped to the barn, and upon our arrival, Holmes did little more than inspect its interior from the entrance. His eyes widened at one point, but otherwise, he remained impassive, as if deep in thought.

I saw nothing amiss. The four horses there appeared in good health.

When we returned to the kitchen, Lestrade spun about and announced over his shoulder his intention of passing the description to London.

"There's no need," my friend said.

With a slow turn, he and glared at Holmes. "And I suppose you know where the man is?"

"No, but I believe Lord Mayweather does."

The earl pulled back his chin, letting his jaw drop slightly. "I, sir? You don't think I took the dog?"

Holmes shook his head. "No, I don't believe you took the dog. However, I do believe you know where Mr. Bristol is."

His features hardened, and he pulled on his shirt cuff. "And what makes you think that, Mr. Holmes?"

"Because, my lord, you had staff escort him from the estate, yet no one seems to know his whereabouts. Not to mention, young Miss Annie here showed a moment of surprise when you described Bristol. I would venture that Bristol is short and thin with light hair and brown eyes. All the leashes were too short for a tall man to use with a dog Lord Boatswain's size." He met the man's gaze, one hard stare to another, and added. "I must say your earlier performance as the concerned husband and dog owner was much more convincing than this current one. Now where did Bristol take Lord Boatswain?"

"Bristol didn't take him anywhere." He slumped into the seat and ran his hands through his hair. "Bristol's in Lady Mayweather's room. Convalescing."

My reaction was only slightly milder than Lestrade's. We both stared at first at the earl and then at Holmes, then back to the earl. Lestrade fingered his darbies, but I could tell the idea of arresting an earl—and for what?—made him hesitate. Before I could ask how Holmes knew this, Annie spoke up again.

"Oh, please, sir, if you're going to arrest someone, let it be me. It were all my fault."

The tears had appeared again on her cheeks, and Willoughby rushed to her side, putting an arm around her shoulders. "No, that's not right. Arrest me."

With the next breath, all the servants held out their hands, offering their wrists. "It was my fault. Arrest me."

Holmes raised a hand, silencing the clamor. "No one is being arrested, are they, Lestrade?"

The poor inspector shifted on his feet and put away his darbies. "I'm trying to see where there was a crime. Unless...Did Lady Mayweather attack Bristol over the chicken bones?"

The earl waved his hand haphazardly. "No. Lord Boatswain bit him when he tried to remove the bone. As I told you, the dog is in a competition next week, and we didn't want anyone to know he might be ill. Lady Mayweather took him to London to see a veterinarian there to confirm there was no permanent damage."

"So, there was no dog-napping?" Lestrade said in a rather gruff voice. "I came all the way out here because of a dog bite?"

Lord Mayweather slumped even further in his chair. "This whole affair has gotten out of hand. I contacted a friend in the Home Office asking him to meet my wife in London and that she was traveling with Lord Boatswain who was ill, but to keep it all hush-hush for security reasons. Somehow the message was misconstrued, and the next thing I know, Inspector Lestrade arrives with a letter of introduction from Mycroft Holmes and a note that his brother Sherlock would be in charge of the search for Lord Boatswain along with Inspector Lestrade. Again, I didn't want it to get out that anything was wrong with Lord Boatswain because of the competition. I thought if we just went along for a bit, until the dog was out of danger, we would announce the dog was found in London and all would be well."

I closed my eyes for the briefest of seconds, as relief swept over me. The dog had not been kidnapped, and no one here would be arrested. No better outcome—except for Bristol. At that thought, I spoke up. "Just to confirm all is well, I would like to examine Mr. Bristol. A dog bite—even from such a well-cared-for animal as Boatswain—should be tended to correctly."

Before I could turn to seek out the dog's trainer, Lestrade said in a firm voice, "Just a minute. We have only your word, my lord, that all's well. How do we even know Lady Mayweather is in London? And if there's been no crime, I could have you arrested for making a false claim."

"Really, Lestrade," Holmes said and made a clucking sound with his tongue. "Have not heard or observed anything while we've been here? If anyone made a false claim, it would have been my brother Mycroft when he fetched you and me down here. And although I would dearly love to hold this over his head for some future favor, I believe the true culprit was the Home Office contact who misunderstood the situation from the beginning.

"Let me review my observations that led me to resolve this situation. Firstly, there were the items missing from Lord Boatswain's room. A leash too short for use by Willoughby, whom you first accused of absconding with the dog, but the proper length for a woman, such as Lady Mayweather. His favorite plaid coat was also missing. Someone who did not care for the dog, such as an actual criminal planning to hold him for ransom, would not have bothered. The comfort of a familiar item such as his favorite coat would have been selected to keep him calm on the trip to London. At that point, I knew there had been no crime, but I wasn't sure exactly all that transpired.

"The incident with the chicken bones, however, provided some indication of what had happened and pointed me in the direction of Mr. Bristol. That no one would provide any information on the man—other than he'd been dismissed—suggested he hadn't left as Lord Mayweather had said. Given that Lady Mayweather was not to be disturbed, I knew that Mr. Bristol had been secreted there for our visit. Furthermore, with her not available for interview and Lord Boatswain's items missing, I knew both she and the dog were not on the estate. When I visited the stables, I already knew feeding the cats chicken bones was not related, but I wanted to see if any horses might be missing. I observed two stalls were empty, but recently used and knew someone (Lady Mayweather and the dog) had left in a carriage.

"The only missing information—the exact location of Lady Mayweather and Lord Boatswain—could be supplied by her husband," he paused and glanced around the room, "or any of those present because when they all confessed to the kidnapping, it was obvious they all knew the true story. You have a very loyal staff, Lord Mayweather. I commend you on your obvious generous nature that would nurture such feelings."

At this compliment, the earl straightened in his seat and nodded at my friend.

Lestrade's shoulders sagged, however, as Holmes' review of the case took all the wind out of his righteous anger. "When you explain it that way...."

"As far as I'm concerned," said my friend, "the case of the missing Lord Boatswain is resolved. You can report so back to my brother and your superiors. If they ask, you can respond that he had suffered an attack and was spirited to London for discretionary treatment. And we'll leave it at that. At least for the time being."

With great effort, I kept my lips from twitching and was grateful for my mustache's cover to keep them hidden. I knew that a time would come when Mycroft's assistance would be needed and Holmes would use his overly enthusiastic response to the earl's request to gain the upper hand on his older brother.

THE DISAPPEARANCE OF LADY FRANCES CARFAX

BY ARTHUR CONAN DOYLE

"*B*ut why Turkish?" asked Mr. Sherlock Holmes, gazing fixedly at my boots. I was reclining in a cane-backed chair at the moment, and my protruded feet had attracted his ever-active attention.

"English," I answered in some surprise. "I got them at Latimer's, in Oxford Street."

Holmes smiled with an expression of weary patience.

"The bath!" he said; "the bath! Why the relaxing and expensive Turkish rather than the invigorating home-made article?"

"Because for the last few days I have been feeling rheumatic and old. A Turkish bath is what we call an alterative in medicine—a fresh starting-point, a cleanser of the system.

"By the way, Holmes," I added, "I have no doubt the connection between my boots and a Turkish bath is a perfectly self-evident one to a logical mind, and yet I should be obliged to you if you would indicate it."

"The train of reasoning is not very obscure, Watson," said Holmes with a mischievous twinkle. "It belongs to the same elementary class of deduction which I should illustrate if I were to ask you who shared your cab in your drive this morning."

"I don't admit that a fresh illustration is an explanation," said I with some asperity.

"Bravo, Watson! A very dignified and logical remonstrance. Let me see, what were the points? Take the last one first—the cab. You observe that you have some splashes on the left sleeve and shoulder of your coat. Had you sat in the centre of a hansom you would probably have had no splashes, and if you had they would certainly have been symmetrical. Therefore it is clear that you sat at the side. Therefore it is equally clear that you had a companion."

"That is very evident."

"Absurdly commonplace, is it not?"

"But the boots and the bath?"

"Equally childish. You are in the habit of doing up your boots in a certain way. I see them on this occasion fastened with an elaborate double bow, which is not your usual method of tying them. You have, therefore, had them off. Who has tied them? A bootmaker—or the boy at the bath. It is unlikely that it is the bootmaker, since your boots are nearly new. Well, what remains? The bath. Absurd, is it not? But, for all that, the Turkish bath has served a purpose."

"What is that?"

"You say that you have had it because you need a change. Let me suggest that you take one. How would Lausanne do, my dear Watson— first-class tickets and all expenses paid on a princely scale?"

"Splendid! But why?"

Holmes leaned back in his armchair and took his notebook from his pocket.

"One of the most dangerous classes in the world," said he, "is the drifting and friendless woman. She is the most harmless and often the most useful of mortals, but she is the inevitable inciter of crime in others. She is helpless. She is migratory. She has sufficient means to take her from country to country and from hotel to hotel. She is lost, as often as not, in a maze of obscure *pensions* and boardinghouses. She is a stray chicken in a world of foxes. When she is gobbled up she is hardly missed. I much fear that some evil has come to the Lady Frances Carfax."

I was relieved at this sudden descent from the general to the particular. Holmes consulted his notes.

"Lady Frances," he continued, "is the sole survivor of the direct family of the late Earl of Rufton. The estates went, as you may remember, in the male line. She was left with limited means, but with some very remarkable old Spanish jewellery of silver and curiously cut diamonds to which she was fondly attached—too attached, for she refused to leave them with her banker and always carried them about with her. A rather pathetic figure, the Lady Frances, a beautiful woman, still in fresh middle age, and yet, by a strange change, the last derelict of what only twenty years ago was a goodly fleet."

"What has happened to her, then?"

"Ah, what has happened to the Lady Frances? Is she alive or dead? There is our problem. She is a lady of precise habits, and for four years it has been her invariable custom to write every second week to Miss Dobney, her old governess, who has long retired and lives in Camberwell. It is this Miss Dobney who has consulted me. Nearly five weeks have passed without a word. The last letter was from the Hôtel National at Lausanne. Lady Frances seems to have left there and given no address. The family are anxious, and as they are exceedingly wealthy no sum will be spared if we can clear the matter up."

"Is Miss Dobney the only source of information? Surely she had other correspondents?"

"There is one correspondent who is a sure draw, Watson. That is the bank. Single ladies must live, and their passbooks are compressed diaries. She banks at Silvester's. I have glanced over her account. The last check but one paid her bill at Lausanne, but it was a large one and probably left her with cash in hand. Only one check has been drawn since."

"To whom, and where?"

"To Miss Marie Devine. There is nothing to show where the check was drawn. It was cashed at the Crédit Lyonnais at Montpellier less than three weeks ago. The sum was fifty pounds."

"And who is Miss Marie Devine?"

"That also I have been able to discover. Miss Marie Devine was the maid of Lady Frances Carfax. Why she should have paid her this check we have not yet determined. I have no doubt, however, that your researches will soon clear the matter up."

"*My* researches!"

"Hence the health-giving expedition to Lausanne. You know that I cannot possibly leave London while old Abrahams is in such mortal terror of his life. Besides, on general principles it is best that I should not leave the country. Scotland Yard feels lonely without me, and it causes an unhealthy excitement among the criminal classes. Go, then, my dear Watson, and if my humble counsel can ever be valued at so extravagant a rate as two pence a word, it waits your disposal night and day at the end of the Continental wire."

TWO DAYS later found me at the Hôtel National at Lausanne, where I received every courtesy at the hands of M. Moser, the well-known manager. Lady Frances, as he informed me, had stayed there for several weeks. She had been much liked by all who met her. Her age was not more than forty. She was still handsome and bore every sign of having in her youth been a very lovely woman. M. Moser knew nothing of any valuable jewellery, but it had been remarked by the servants that the heavy trunk in the lady's bedroom was always scrupulously locked. Marie Devine, the maid, was as popular as her mistress. She was actually engaged to one of the head waiters in the hotel, and there was no difficulty in getting her address. It was 11, Rue de Trajan, Montpellier. All this I jotted down and felt that Holmes himself could not have been more adroit in collecting his facts.

Only one corner still remained in the shadow. No light which I possessed could clear up the cause for the lady's sudden departure. She was very happy at Lausanne. There was every reason to believe that she intended to remain for the season in her luxurious rooms overlooking the lake. And yet she had left at a single day's notice, which involved her in the useless payment of a week's rent. Only Jules Vibart, the lover of the maid, had any suggestion to offer. He connected the sudden departure with the visit to the hotel a day or two before of a tall, dark, bearded man. "*Un sauvage—un veritable sauvage!"* cried Jules Vibart. The man had rooms somewhere in the town. He had been seen talking earnestly to Madame on the promenade by the lake. Then he had called. She had refused to see him. He was English, but of his name there was no record. Madame had left the place immediately afterwards. Jules Vibart, and, what was of more importance, Jules Vibart's sweetheart, thought that this call and the departure were cause and effect. Only one thing Jules would not discuss. That was the reason why Marie had left her mistress. Of that he could or would say nothing. If I wished to know, I must go to Montpellier and ask her.

So ended the first chapter of my inquiry. The second was devoted to the place which Lady Frances Carfax had sought when she left Lausanne. Concerning this there had been some secrecy, which confirmed the idea that she had gone with the intention of throwing someone off her track. Otherwise why should not her luggage have been openly labelled for Baden? Both she and it reached the Rhenish spa by some circuitous route. This much I gathered from the manager of Cook's local office. So to Baden I went, after dispatching to Holmes an account of all my proceedings and receiving in reply a telegram of half-humorous commendation.

At Baden the track was not difficult to follow. Lady Frances had stayed at the Englischer Hof for a fortnight. While there she had made the acquaintance of a Dr. Shlessinger and his wife, a missionary from South America. Like most lonely ladies, Lady Frances found her comfort and occupation in religion. Dr. Shlessinger's remarkable personality, his whole hearted devotion, and the fact that he was recovering from a disease contracted in the exercise of his apostolic duties affected her deeply. She had helped Mrs. Shlessinger in the nursing of the convalescent saint. He spent his day, as the manager described it to me, upon a lounge-chair on the veranda, with an attendant lady upon either side of him. He was preparing a map of the Holy Land, with special reference to the kingdom of the Midianites, upon which he was writing a monograph. Finally, having improved much in health, he and his wife had returned to London, and Lady Frances had started thither in their company. This was just three weeks before, and the manager had heard nothing since. As to the maid, Marie, she had gone off some days beforehand in floods of tears, after informing the other maids that she was leaving service forever. Dr. Shlessinger had paid the bill of the whole party before his departure.

"By the way," said the landlord in conclusion, "you are not the only friend of Lady Frances Carfax who is inquiring after her just now. Only a week or so ago we had a man here upon the same errand."

"Did he give a name?" I asked.

"None; but he was an Englishman, though of an unusual type."

"A savage?" said I, linking my facts after the fashion of my illustrious friend.

"Exactly. That describes him very well. He is a bulky, bearded, sunburned fellow, who looks as if he would be more at home in a farmers' inn than in a fashionable hotel. A hard, fierce man, I should think, and one whom I should be sorry to offend."

Already the mystery began to define itself, as figures grow clearer with the lifting of a fog. Here was this good and pious lady pursued from place to place by a sinister and unrelenting figure. She feared him, or she would not have fled from Lausanne. He had still followed. Sooner or later he would overtake her. Had he already overtaken her? Was *that* the secret of her continued silence? Could the good people who were her companions not screen her from his violence or his blackmail? What horrible purpose, what deep design, lay behind this long pursuit? There was the problem which I had to solve.

To Holmes I wrote showing how rapidly and surely I had got down to the roots of the matter. In reply I had a telegram asking for a description of Dr. Shlessinger's left ear. Holmes's ideas of humour are strange and occasionally offensive, so I took no notice of his ill-timed jest—indeed, I had already reached Montpellier in my pursuit of the maid, Marie, before his message came.

I had no difficulty in finding the ex-servant and in learning all that she could tell me. She was a devoted creature, who had only left her mistress because she was sure that she was in good hands, and because her own approaching marriage made a separation inevitable in any case. Her mistress had, as she confessed with distress, shown some irritability of temper towards her during their stay in Baden, and had even questioned her once as if she had suspicions of her honesty, and this had made the parting easier than it would otherwise have been. Lady Frances had given her fifty pounds as a wedding-present. Like me, Marie viewed with deep distrust the stranger who had driven her mistress from Lausanne. With her own eyes she had seen him seize the lady's wrist with great violence on the public promenade by the lake. He was a fierce and terrible man. She believed that it was out of dread of him that Lady Frances had accepted the escort of the Shlessingers to London. She had never spoken to Marie about it, but many little signs had convinced the maid that her mistress lived in a state of continual nervous apprehension. So far she had got in her narrative, when suddenly she sprang from her chair and her face was convulsed with surprise and fear. "See!" she cried. "The miscreant follows still! There is the very man of whom I speak."

Through the open sitting-room window I saw a huge, swarthy man with a bristling black beard walking slowly down the centre of the street and staring eagerly at the numbers of the houses. It was clear that, like myself, he was on the track of the maid. Acting upon the impulse of the moment, I rushed out and accosted him.

"You are an Englishman," I said.

"What if I am?" he asked with a most villainous scowl.

"May I ask what your name is?"

"No, you may not," said he with decision.

The situation was awkward, but the most direct way is often the best.

"Where is the Lady Frances Carfax?" I asked.

He stared at me with amazement.

"What have you done with her? Why have you pursued her? I insist upon an answer!" said I.

The fellow gave a bellow of anger and sprang upon me like a tiger. I have held my own in many a struggle, but the man had a grip of iron and the fury of a fiend. His hand was on my throat and my senses were nearly gone before an unshaven French *ouvrier* in a blue blouse darted out from a *cabaret* opposite, with a cudgel in his hand, and struck my assailant a sharp crack over the forearm, which made him leave go his hold. He stood for an instant fuming with rage and uncertain whether he should not renew his attack. Then, with a snarl of anger, he left me and entered the cottage from which I had just come. I turned to thank my preserver, who stood beside me in the roadway.

"Well, Watson," said he, "a very pretty hash you have made of it! I rather think you had better come back with me to London by the night express."

An hour afterwards, Sherlock Holmes, in his usual garb and style, was seated in my private room at the hotel. His explanation of his sudden and opportune appearance was simplicity itself, for, finding that he could get away from London, he determined to head me off at the next obvious point of my travels. In the disguise of a workingman he had sat in the *cabaret* waiting for my appearance.

"And a singularly consistent investigation you have made, my dear Watson," said he. "I cannot at the moment recall any possible blunder which you have omitted. The total effect of your proceeding has been to give the alarm everywhere and yet to discover nothing."

"Perhaps you would have done no better," I answered bitterly.

"There is no 'perhaps' about it. I *have* done better. Here is the Hon. Philip Green, who is a fellow-lodger with you in this hotel, and we may find him the starting-point for a more successful investigation."

A card had come up on a salver, and it was followed by the same bearded ruffian who had attacked me in the street. He started when he saw me.

"What is this, Mr. Holmes?" he asked. "I had your note and I have come. But what has this man to do with the matter?"

"This is my old friend and associate, Dr. Watson, who is helping us in this affair."

The stranger held out a huge, sunburned hand, with a few words of apology.

"I hope I didn't harm you. When you accused me of hurting her I lost my grip of myself. Indeed, I'm not responsible in these days. My nerves are like live wires. But this situation is beyond me. What I want to know, in the first place, Mr. Holmes, is, how in the world you came to hear of my existence at all."

"I am in touch with Miss Dobney, Lady Frances's governess."

"Old Susan Dobney with the mob cap! I remember her well."

"And she remembers you. It was in the days before—before you found it better to go to South Africa."

"Ah, I see you know my whole story. I need hide nothing from you. I swear to you, Mr. Holmes, that there never was in this world a man who loved a woman with a more wholehearted love than I had for Frances. I was a wild youngster, I know—not worse than others of my class. But her mind was pure as snow. She could not bear a shadow of coarseness. So, when she came to hear of things that I had done, she would have no more to say to me. And yet she loved me—that is the wonder of it!—loved me well enough to remain single all her sainted days just for my sake alone. When the years had passed and I had made my money at Barberton I thought perhaps I could seek her out and soften her. I had heard that she was still unmarried, I found her at Lausanne and tried all I knew. She weakened, I think, but her will was strong, and when next I called she had left the town. I traced her to Baden, and then after a time heard that her maid was here. I'm a rough fellow, fresh from a rough life, and when Dr. Watson spoke to me as he did I lost hold of myself for a moment. But for God's sake tell me what has become of the Lady Frances."

"That is for us to find out," said Sherlock Holmes with peculiar gravity. "What is your London address, Mr. Green?"

"The Langham Hotel will find me."

"Then may I recommend that you return there and be on hand in case I should want you? I have no desire to encourage false hopes, but you may rest assured that all that can be done will be done for the safety of Lady Frances. I can say no more for the instant. I will leave you this card so that you may be able to keep in touch with us. Now, Watson, if you will pack your bag I will cable to Mrs. Hudson to make one of her best efforts for two hungry travellers at 7:30 to-morrow."

A telegram was awaiting us when we reached our Baker Street rooms, which Holmes read with an exclamation of interest and threw across to me. "Jagged or torn," was the message, and the place of origin, Baden.

"What is this?" I asked.

"It is everything," Holmes answered. "You may remember my seemingly irrelevant question as to this clerical gentleman's left ear. You did not answer it."

"I had left Baden and could not inquire."

"Exactly. For this reason I sent a duplicate to the manager of the Englischer Hof, whose answer lies here." "What does it show?"

"It shows, my dear Watson, that we are dealing with an exceptionally astute and dangerous man. The Rev. Dr. Shlessinger, missionary from South America, is none other than Holy Peters, one of the most unscrupulous rascals that Australia has ever evolved—and for a young country it has turned out some very finished types. His particular specialty is the beguiling of lonely ladies by playing upon their religious feelings, and his so-called wife, an Englishwoman named Fraser, is a worthy helpmate. The nature of his tactics suggested his identity to me, and this physical peculiarity—he was badly bitten in a saloon-fight at Adelaide in '89—confirmed my suspicion. This poor lady is in the hands of a most infernal couple, who will stick at nothing, Watson. That she is already dead is a very likely supposition. If not, she is undoubtedly in some sort of confinement and unable to write to Miss Dobney or her other friends. It is always possible that she never reached London, or that she has passed through it, but the former is improbable, as, with their system of registration, it is not easy for foreigners to play tricks with the Continental police; and the latter is also unlikely, as these rogues could not hope to find any other place where it would be as easy to keep a person under restraint. All my instincts tell me that she is in London, but as we have at present no possible means of telling where, we can only take the obvious steps, eat our dinner, and possess our souls in patience. Later in the evening I will stroll down and have a word with friend Lestrade at Scotland Yard."

But neither the official police nor Holmes's own small but very efficient organisation sufficed to clear away the mystery. Amid the crowded millions of London the three persons we sought were as completely obliterated as if they had never lived. Advertisements were tried, and failed. Clues were followed, and led to nothing. Every criminal resort which Shlessinger might frequent was drawn in vain. His old associates were watched, but they kept clear of him. And then suddenly, after a week of helpless suspense there came a flash of light. A silver-and-brilliant pendant of old Spanish design had been pawned at Bovington's, in Westminster Road. The pawner was a large, clean-shaven man of clerical appearance. His name and address were demonstrably false. The ear had escaped notice, but the description was surely that of Shlessinger.

Three times had our bearded friend from the Langham called for news —the third time within an hour of this fresh development. His clothes were getting looser on his great body. He seemed to be wilting away in his anxiety. "If you will only give me something to do!" was his constant wail. At last Holmes could oblige him.

"He has begun to pawn the jewels. We should get him now."

"But does this mean that any harm has befallen the Lady Frances?"

Holmes shook his head very gravely.

"Supposing that they have held her prisoner up to now, it is clear that they cannot let her loose without their own destruction. We must prepare for the worst."

"What can I do?"

"These people do not know you by sight?" "No."

"It is possible that he will go to some other pawnbroker in the future. In that case, we must begin again. On the other hand, he has had a fair price and no questions asked, so if he is in need of ready-money he will probably come back to Bovington's. I will give you a note to them, and they will let you wait in the shop. If the fellow comes you will follow him home. But no indiscretion, and, above all, no violence. I put you on your honour that you will take no step without my knowledge and consent."

For two days the Hon. Philip Green (he was, I may mention, the son of the famous admiral of that name who commanded the Sea of Azof fleet in the Crimean War) brought us no news. On the evening of the third he rushed into our sitting-room, pale, trembling, with every muscle of his powerful frame quivering with excitement.

"We have him! We have him!" he cried.

He was incoherent in his agitation. Holmes soothed him with a few words and thrust him into an armchair.

"Come, now, give us the order of events," said he.

"She came only an hour ago. It was the wife, this time, but the pendant she brought was the fellow of the other. She is a tall, pale woman, with ferret eyes."

"That is the lady," said Holmes.

"She left the office and I followed her. She walked up the Kennington Road, and I kept behind her. Presently she went into a shop. Mr. Holmes, it was an undertaker's."

My companion started. "Well?" he asked in that vibrant voice which told of the fiery soul behind the cold grey face.

"She was talking to the woman behind the counter. I entered as well. 'It is late,' I heard her say, or words to that effect. The woman was excusing herself. 'It should be there before now,' she answered. 'It took longer, being out of the ordinary.' They both stopped and looked at me, so I asked some questions and then left the shop."

"You did excellently well. What happened next?"

"The woman came out, but I had hid myself in a doorway. Her suspicions had been aroused, I think, for she looked round her. Then she called a cab and got in. I was lucky enough to get another and so to follow her. She got down at last at No. 36, Poultney Square, Brixton. I drove past, left my cab at the corner of the square, and watched the house."

"Did you see anyone?"

"The windows were all in darkness save one on the lower floor. The blind was down, and I could not see in. I was standing there, wondering what I should do next, when a covered van drove up with two men in it. They descended, took something out of the van, and carried it up the steps to the hall door. Mr. Holmes, it was a coffin."

"Ah!"

"For an instant I was on the point of rushing in. The door had been opened to admit the men and their burden. It was the woman who had opened it. But as I stood there she caught a glimpse of me, and I think that she recognised me. I saw her start, and she hastily closed the door. I remembered my promise to you, and here I am."

"You have done excellent work," said Holmes, scribbling a few words upon a half-sheet of paper. "We can do nothing legal without a warrant, and you can serve the cause best by taking this note down to the authorities and getting one. There may be some difficulty, but I should think that the sale of the jewellery should be sufficient. Lestrade will see to all details."

"But they may murder her in the meanwhile. What could the coffin mean, and for whom could it be but for her?"

"We will do all that can be done, Mr. Green. Not a moment will be lost. Leave it in our hands. Now, Watson," he added as our client hurried away, "he will set the regular forces on the move. We are, as usual, the irregulars, and we must take our own line of action. The situation strikes me as so desperate that the most extreme measures are justified. Not a moment is to be lost in getting to Poultney Square.

"Let us try to reconstruct the situation," said he as we drove swiftly past the Houses of Parliament and over Westminster Bridge. "These villains have coaxed this unhappy lady to London, after first alienating her from her faithful maid. If she has written any letters they have been intercepted. Through some confederate they have engaged a furnished house. Once inside it, they have made her a prisoner, and they have become possessed of the valuable jewellery which has been their object from the first. Already they have begun to sell part of it, which seems safe enough to them, since they have no reason to think that anyone is interested in the lady's fate. When she is released she will, of course, denounce them. Therefore, she must not be released. But they cannot keep her under lock and key forever. So murder is their only solution."

"That seems very clear."

"Now we will take another line of reasoning. When you follow two separate chains of thought, Watson, you will find some point of intersection which should approximate to the truth. We will start now, not from the lady but from the coffin and argue backward. That incident proves, I fear, beyond all doubt that the lady is dead. It points also to an orthodox burial with proper accompaniment of medical certificate and official sanction. Had the lady been obviously murdered, they would have buried her in a hole in the back garden. But here all is open and regular. What does this mean? Surely that they have done her to death in some way which has deceived the doctor and simulated a natural end—poisoning, perhaps. And yet how strange that they should ever let a doctor approach her unless he were a confederate, which is hardly a credible proposition."

"Could they have forged a medical certificate?"

"Dangerous, Watson, very dangerous. No, I hardly see them doing that.

Pull up, cabby! This is evidently the undertaker's, for we have just passed the pawnbroker's. Would you go in, Watson? Your appearance inspires confidence. Ask what hour the Poultney Square funeral takes place to-morrow."

The woman in the shop answered me without hesitation that it was to be at eight o'clock in the morning. "You see, Watson, no mystery; everything above-board! In some way the legal forms have undoubtedly been complied with, and they think that they have little to fear. Well, there's nothing for it now but a direct frontal attack. Are you armed?"

"My stick!"

"Well, well, we shall be strong enough. 'Thrice is he armed who hath his quarrel just.' We simply can't afford to wait for the police or to keep within the four corners of the law. You can drive off, cabby. Now, Watson, we'll just take our luck together, as we have occasionally in the past."

He had rung loudly at the door of a great dark house in the centre of Poultney Square. It was opened immediately, and the figure of a tall woman was outlined against the dim-lit hall.

"Well, what do you want?" she asked sharply, peering at us through the darkness.

"I want to speak to Dr. Shlessinger," said Holmes.

"There is no such person here," she answered, and tried to close the door, but Holmes had jammed it with his foot.

"Well, I want to see the man who lives here, whatever he may call himself," said Holmes firmly.

She hesitated. Then she threw open the door. "Well, come in!" said she. "My husband is not afraid to face any man in the world." She closed the door behind us and showed us into a sitting-room on the right side of the hall, turning up the gas as she left us. "Mr. Peters will be with you in an instant," she said.

Her words were literally true, for we had hardly time to look around the dusty and moth-eaten apartment in which we found ourselves before the door opened and a big, clean-shaven bald-headed man stepped lightly into the room. He had a large red face, with pendulous cheeks, and a general air of superficial benevolence which was marred by a cruel, vicious mouth.

"There is surely some mistake here, gentlemen," he said in an unctuous, make-everything-easy voice. "I fancy that you have been misdirected. Possibly if you tried farther down the street—"

"That will do; we have no time to waste," said my companion firmly. "You are Henry Peters, of Adelaide, late the Rev. Dr. Shlessinger, of Baden and South America. I am as sure of that as that my own name is Sherlock Holmes."

Peters, as I will now call him, started and stared hard at his formidable pursuer. "I guess your name does not frighten me, Mr. Holmes," said he coolly. "When a man's conscience is easy you can't rattle him. What is your business in my house?"

"I want to know what you have done with the Lady Frances Carfax, whom you brought away with you from Baden."

"I'd be very glad if you could tell me where that lady may be," Peters answered coolly. "I've a bill against her for nearly a hundred pounds, and nothing to show for it but a couple of trumpery pendants that the dealer would hardly look at. She attached herself to Mrs. Peters and me at Baden —it is a fact that I was using another name at the time—and she stuck on to us until we came to London. I paid her bill and her ticket. Once in London, she gave us the slip, and, as I say, left these out-of-date jewels to pay her bills. You find her, Mr. Holmes, and I'm your debtor."

"I *mean* to find her," said Sherlock Holmes. "I'm going through this house till I do find her."

"Where is your warrant?"

Holmes half drew a revolver from his pocket. "This will have to serve till a better one comes."

"Why, you're a common burglar."

"So you might describe me," said Holmes cheerfully. "My companion is also a dangerous ruffian. And together we are going through your house."

Our opponent opened the door.

"Fetch a policeman, Annie!" said he. There was a whisk of feminine skirts down the passage, and the hall door was opened and shut.

"Our time is limited, Watson," said Holmes. "If you try to stop us, Peters, you will most certainly get hurt. Where is that coffin which was brought into your house?"

"What do you want with the coffin? It is in use. There is a body in it."

"I must see the body."

"Never with my consent."

"Then without it." With a quick movement Holmes pushed the fellow to one side and passed into the hall. A door half opened stood immediately before us. We entered. It was the dining-room. On the table, under a half-lit chandelier, the coffin was lying. Holmes turned up the gas and raised the lid. Deep down in the recesses of the coffin lay an emaciated figure. The glare from the lights above beat down upon an aged and withered face. By no possible process of cruelty, starvation, or disease could this worn-out wreck be the still beautiful Lady Frances. Holmes's face showed his amazement, and also his relief.

"Thank God!" he muttered. "It's someone else."

"Ah, you've blundered badly for once, Mr. Sherlock Holmes," said Peters, who had followed us into the room.

"Who is the dead woman?"

"Well, if you really must know, she is an old nurse of my wife's, Rose Spender by name, whom we found in the Brixton Workhouse Infirmary. We brought her round here, called in Dr. Horsom, of 13, Firbank Villas—mind you take the address, Mr. Holmes—and had her carefully tended, as Christian folk should. On the third day she died—certificate says senile decay—but that's only the doctor's opinion, and of course you know better. We ordered her funeral to be carried out by Stimson and Co., of the Kennington Road, who will bury her at eight o'clock to-morrow morning. Can you pick any hole in that, Mr. Holmes? You've made a silly blunder, and you may as well own up to it. I'd give something for a photograph of your gaping, staring face when you pulled aside that lid expecting to see the Lady Frances Carfax and only found a poor old woman of ninety."

Holmes's expression was as impassive as ever under the jeers of his antagonist, but his clenched hands betrayed his acute annoyance.

"I am going through your house," said he.

"Are you, though!" cried Peters as a woman's voice and heavy steps sounded in the passage. "We'll soon see about that. This way, officers, if you please. These men have forced their way into my house, and I cannot get rid of them. Help me to put them out."

A sergeant and a constable stood in the doorway. Holmes drew his card from his case.

"This is my name and address. This is my friend, Dr. Watson."

"Bless you, sir, we know you very well," said the sergeant, "but you can't stay here without a warrant."

"Of course not. I quite understand that."

"Arrest him!" cried Peters.

"We know where to lay our hands on this gentleman if he is wanted," said the sergeant majestically, "but you'll have to go, Mr. Holmes."

"Yes, Watson, we shall have to go."

A minute later we were in the street once more. Holmes was as cool as ever, but I was hot with anger and humiliation. The sergeant had followed us.

"Sorry, Mr. Holmes, but that's the law."

"Exactly, Sergeant, you could not do otherwise."

"I expect there was good reason for your presence there. If there is anything I can do—"

"It's a missing lady, Sergeant, and we think she is in that house. I expect a warrant presently."

"Then I'll keep my eye on the parties, Mr. Holmes. If anything comes along, I will surely let you know."

It was only nine o'clock, and we were off full cry upon the trail at once. First we drove to Brixton Workhouse Infirmary, where we found that it was indeed the truth that a charitable couple had called some days before, that they had claimed an imbecile old woman as a former servant, and that they had obtained permission to take her away with them. No surprise was expressed at the news that she had since died.

The doctor was our next goal. He had been called in, had found the woman dying of pure senility, had actually seen her pass away, and had signed the certificate in due form. "I assure you that everything was perfectly normal and there was no room for foul play in the matter," said he. Nothing in the house had struck him as suspicious save that for people of their class it was remarkable that they should have no servant. So far and no further went the doctor.

Finally we found our way to Scotland Yard. There had been difficulties of procedure in regard to the warrant. Some delay was inevitable. The magistrate's signature might not be obtained until next morning. If Holmes would call about nine he could go down with Lestrade and see it acted upon. So ended the day, save that near midnight our friend, the sergeant, called to say that he had seen flickering lights here and there in the windows of the great dark house, but that no one had left it and none had entered. We could but pray for patience and wait for the morrow.

Sherlock Holmes was too irritable for conversation and too restless for sleep. I left him smoking hard, with his heavy, dark brows knotted together, and his long, nervous fingers tapping upon the arms of his chair, as he turned over in his mind every possible solution of the mystery. Several times in the course of the night I heard him prowling about the house. Finally, just after I had been called in the morning, he rushed into my room. He was in his dressing-gown, but his pale, hollow-eyed face told me that his night had been a sleepless one.

"What time was the funeral? Eight, was it not?" he asked eagerly. "Well, it is 7:20 now. Good heavens, Watson, what has become of any brains that God has given me? Quick, man, quick! It's life or death—a hundred chances on death to one on life. I'll never forgive myself, never, if we are too late!"

Five minutes had not passed before we were flying in a hansom down Baker Street. But even so it was twenty-five to eight as we passed Big Ben, and eight struck as we tore down the Brixton Road. But others were late as well as we. Ten minutes after the hour the hearse was still standing at the door of the house, and even as our foaming horse came to a halt the coffin, supported by three men, appeared on the threshold. Holmes darted forward and barred their way.

"Take it back!" he cried, laying his hand on the breast of the foremost. "Take it back this instant!"

"What the devil do you mean? Once again I ask you, where is your warrant?" shouted the furious Peters, his big red face glaring over the farther end of the coffin.

"The warrant is on its way. The coffin shall remain in the house until it comes."

The authority in Holmes's voice had its effect upon the bearers. Peters had suddenly vanished into the house, and they obeyed these new orders. "Quick, Watson, quick! Here is a screw-driver!" he shouted as the coffin was replaced upon the table. "Here's one for you, my man! A sovereign if the lid comes off in a minute! Ask no questions—work away! That's good! Another! And another! Now pull all together! It's giving! It's giving! Ah, that does it at last."

With a united effort we tore off the coffin-lid. As we did so there came from the inside a stupefying and overpowering smell of chloroform. A body lay within, its head all wreathed in cotton-wool, which had been soaked in the narcotic. Holmes plucked it off and disclosed the statuesque face of a handsome and spiritual woman of middle age. In an instant he had passed his arm round the figure and raised her to a sitting position.

"Is she gone, Watson? Is there a spark left? Surely we are not too late!"

For half an hour it seemed that we were. What with actual suffocation, and what with the poisonous fumes of the chloroform, the Lady Frances seemed to have passed the last point of recall. And then, at last, with artificial respiration, with injected ether, and with every device that science could suggest, some flutter of life, some quiver of the eyelids, some dimming of a mirror, spoke of the slowly returning life. A cab had driven up, and Holmes, parting the blind, looked out at it. "Here is Lestrade with his warrant," said he. "He will find that his birds have flown. And here," he added as a heavy step hurried along the passage, "is someone who has a better right to nurse this lady than we have. Good morning, Mr. Green; I think that the sooner we can move the Lady Frances the better. Meanwhile, the funeral may proceed, and the poor old woman who still lies in that coffin may go to her last resting-place alone."

"Should you care to add the case to your annals, my dear Watson," said Holmes that evening, "it can only be as an example of that temporary eclipse to which even the best-balanced mind may be exposed. Such slips are common to all mortals, and the greatest is he who can recognise and repair them. To this modified credit I may, perhaps, make some claim. My night was haunted by the thought that somewhere a clue, a strange sentence, a curious observation, had come under my notice and had been too easily dismissed. Then, suddenly, in the grey of the morning, the words came back to me. It was the remark of the undertaker's wife, as reported by Philip Green. She had said, 'It should be there before now. It took longer, being out of the ordinary.' It was the coffin of which she spoke. It had been out of the ordinary. That could only mean that it had been made to some special measurement. But why? Why? Then in an instant I remembered the deep sides, and the little wasted figure at the bottom. Why so large a coffin for so small a body? To leave room for another body. Both would be buried under the one certificate. It had all been so clear, if only my own sight had not been dimmed. At eight the Lady Frances would be buried. Our one chance was to stop the coffin before it left the house.

"It was a desperate chance that we might find her alive, but it *was* a chance, as the result showed. These people had never, to my knowledge, done a murder. They might shrink from actual violence at the last. The could bury her with no sign of how she met her end, and even if she were exhumed there was a chance for them. I hoped that such considerations might prevail with them. You can reconstruct the scene well enough. You saw the horrible den upstairs, where the poor lady had been kept so long. They rushed in and overpowered her with their chloroform, carried her down, poured more into the coffin to insure against her waking, and then screwed down the lid. A clever device, Watson. It is new to me in the annals of crime. If our ex-missionary friends escape the clutches of Lestrade, I shall expect to hear of some brilliant incidents in their future career."

THE RETURN OF LADY FRANCES
CARFAX

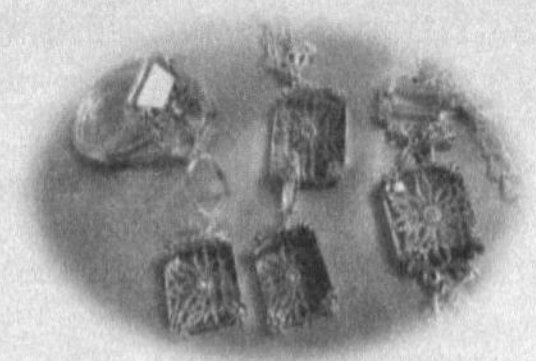

"*A*re you aware of the old Oriental saying about saving a person's life?" the Lady Frances Carfax asked.

The woman sat on the edge of the basket chair my friend Sherlock Holmes always reserved for clients, her spine as rigid as a soldier's at attention. Many of those who sought his assistance would slump forward or recline backward, appearing unable to bear the weight of whatever misfortune had befallen them. The Lady Frances' breeding, however, ensured her composure didn't waiver, regardless of life's vicissitudes.

Holmes had been silent to this point, listening with his fingertips pressed together as she outlined her predicament. Now, he drew in a breath and asked, "You mean the one about the savior having responsibility for the victim for the rest of his or her life?"

"Precisely." If possible, she pulled herself even straighter in the chair. "*You* saved my life." She raised her hand to prevent anyone from protesting the fact. "I know the police were involved, and Dr. Watson here supervised my immediate recovery, but had you not stopped the Shlessingers—"

"You mean Henry Peters and Annie Fraser," he said, focusing on her over his fingertips.

She glared back at him. "You will excuse me if I find it hard to recall their true names. I only ever knew them as Shlessinger. Even after…." She gulped, the first crack in her self-control, no doubt based on her memory of lying in a coffin with a dead woman. "After everything."

With a deep breath to re-establish herself, she continued. "The police have been unable to locate the Shle—er, Peters and Fraser—or recover my jewels. Those two thieves have left me nearly penniless. You saved my life then; now, save me from my current existence. My choices are few: throw myself on the mercy of my cousin—the current Earl of Rufton—who doesn't even answer my letters; move in with my old governess Miss Dobney; or seek some means to support myself on my own."

After a pause, he stated her true request. "You wish me to find your jewels."

"It is your responsibility. Your duty. To me. Otherwise, any misfortune that overtakes me will fall on your shoulders."

I shifted uneasily in my own seat, recalling my friend's observation about an unmarried woman with means being helpless. The statement, made when he first took the case, now carried even greater insight into a single woman's fate. With funds, she was almost entirely defenseless against those who would part her from her fortune. Without them, she lacked even the most rudimentary capacity to care for herself.

"What of the pieces recovered from the pawnbrokers? Your bank account?" I asked, hoping she might have sufficient funds to keep her in a very modest lifestyle.

"The pieces were minor and if sold, along with what is left in my bank, I might be able to live in a hotel for perhaps six months, but then…."

She raised her hands, palms up, as if questioning her future.

"You haven't mentioned the Hon. Philip Green," he said.

"And I won't." Her voice displayed a tinge of disdain toward her former suitor. "Money can't cure all ills. He may have found good luck in South Africa, but that doesn't polish his manners. He is a ruffian and will be for the rest of his life."

He pulled himself from his seat and offered a hand to assist the woman from hers. "Very well, Lady Frances. As you have pointed out, I do have a responsibility in this matter. Please allow me a day or two to resolve some of my current cases, and I will consider how best to proceed with regard to your situation. Where can we reach you at present?"

"You can contact me at Miss Dobney's residence. I understand you have the address. She was kind enough to nurse me through my recovery after I left the hospital. I must economize, given my present state."

Following her exit, I watched a smile play on my friend's lips. "We're in a most curious situation. While I might be able to find Peters and Fraser, and even reclaim her jewels, I'm not certain that her condition would be improved. Are we not only setting her up as bait for some other devious thief? Perhaps there is a better approach…."

"Train her for some employable position?" I asked and recalled the cases where we had encountered those making their own way in the world. "I suppose she might find work as a governess. Or perhaps she could learn to be a typewriter?"

He waved his hands as if to wipe away my words. "Etiquette lessons. The woman would be perfect for helping the less adept at learning proper manners. And I already have her first pupil."

"You're not considering…? Surely, she'd refuse to tutor…?" I couldn't even complete the thought. I shook my head. "The poor man."

"I'd hardly call Philip Green 'poor.' 'Rough,' perhaps. He comes from good stock and made a fortune in South Africa. Like the diamonds from that region, he just needs a little polish. All Green and the Lady Frances require is a reason to refine his manners, which I will give them."

I would have chosen a much stronger word than "rough" to describe the man. He'd nearly throttled me to death.

"A *lot* of polish if you ask me," I muttered.

"At least half of our task is done. He has already professed his feelings toward the lady and would be quite willing to do whatever is asked of him, especially if he can be close to the Lady Frances. Of course, neither can suspect they are being manipulated. The first step is a visit to the telegraph office and then Scotland Yard."

Lestrade scratched his head when Holmes put the question before him. "Why are you so interested in this pair? We haven't heard from them since they got away from us while we were reviving the Lady Frances."

"The victim has employed me to find the rest of her jewels. They hold both monetary as well as sentimental value for her. I feel some moral responsibility for their loss when the thieves made their escape." He met the inspector's gaze. "You have no clues as to their whereabouts?"

"At the time, I told you they most likely left the country. We did check the passenger's logs and found no one named Peters or Shlessinger listed, but that doesn't mean they couldn't have used another name. They could be anywhere. The Continent. Australia. Who knows?"

"I beg to differ," Holmes said, a grim smile on his face. "It's not as easy as one would assume to create a new identity for leaving the country. It takes funds, and while they may have Lady Frances' jewels, these have not appeared in any pawnshops. I've checked. I have, however, placed advertisements in all the major regional papers seeking to purchase such jewels. We may have to wait a day or two, but I have no doubt this pair is reaching the limits of their current funds and have a strong desire to replenish them."

TWO DAYS LATER, both Mr. Green and the Lady Frances were seated next to each other on a couch in 221B. Holmes and Mrs. Hudson had tidied and prepared the room, even setting a bowl of jasmine and lavender blossoms on the table in front of the sofa. The flowers' scent was a pleasant change from the room's normal aroma of stale tobacco. The Lady Frances had given a little sniff when she'd been directed to the spot next to her former suitor, but the man simply smiled in response. Despite my rather rocky introduction to the man, I did have to admit a more loyal fellow to a former lover could not be found in the whole country.

"While I have agreed to take on the task of recovering Lady Frances' jewels, I've asked you here today to request your assistance in this endeavor. My current caseload is very demanding, and I will need your assistance in completing a subterfuge that I am certain will result in their return. I am pleased to report I have located Henry Peters and Annie Fraser. I placed an advertisement in all the major newspapers seeking antique jewels for purchase. While I had several respondents, only one, a Mr. Burton of Birmingham provided a description of the type of jewelry that seemed to fit the missing pieces. After additional correspondence, Mr. Burton agreed to come to London to show them to a Mr. Ronald Henderson, antique enthusiast and collector of rare gems. Burton and his sister will be here in three days. Because Peters and Fraser know my identity, as well as Dr. Watson's, we require another man to pose as Mr. Henderson. I'm asking for your help, Mr. Green. Are you up to the task?"

"I'm game," the man said, rubbing his hands together. "I can't wait to get my hands on those villains. They won't leave in one piece unless they cough up them jewels."

At this pronouncement, the woman stood and pointed to him. "This charade will never work. How can you expect a man of this...this course nature to pass as a refined gentleman of taste? They will see right through the scheme, disappear, and I'll lose all hope of my independence."

She might as well have slapped him. Instead of disputing her depiction of him, he dropped his head in humble acceptance. Before I could go to his defense, my friend spoke up.

"I have learned that manners are one of the more easily adjusted traits and will create an illusion that most unsavory characters will never penetrate. We have three days in which to transform our Mr. Green. And you, Lady Frances, will play a key part in his instruction."

"I?" the woman asked, pulling back her chin. After a moment's thought, she said, "I suppose I *am* the most knowledgeable about proper manners. That is, if Mr. Green will agree to accept my tutoring."

The man nodded vigorously. "Of course. I will do my utmost to become the gentleman you desire."

The lady gave a small noise of derision in the back of her throat but didn't protest.

"Dr. Watson and I will ensure he looks the part. We'll visit a tailor to outfit him, and, with a proper shave and haircut, I daresay even his own mother wouldn't recognize him."

Green opened his mouth as if to object, glanced at the love of his life and snapped it shut. His willingness to endure any and all vexations for her was beyond admirable.

By the day of the meeting with Mr. and Miss Burton, all had been arranged. True to his word, Holmes and the Lady Frances had created a physical transformation of the ruffian into a stately gentleman. Other than his broad shoulders, the man had little in common with the one who'd accosted me on the streets of Montpellier.

Could he, however, deceive a deceiver? Or would Peters/Burton see through the polished veneer he now displayed?

The proof, as they say, would be in the pudding.

Holmes had arranged for a suite in a hotel near Baker Street. The Lady Frances, Holmes, and I hid behind the door to an inner room to listen to Green's meeting with the thieves. At first, all occurred as Holmes had predicted and rehearsed with Green.

`   "You can see these are quite beautiful pieces," Peters said, bringing out one for Green to examine.

"Yes, and quite old," Green said. "But I was taken to believe you had more and larger items."

"This is just a sampling, of course. I have a full list here for you to review."

"I would like to have another jeweler examine them to ensure their value. Do you mind if I keep this piece to do so?"

"These are quite special pieces, as you can see," Miss Fraser/Burton said, speaking for the first time. "They have been in my family for generations."

At this remark, the Lady Frances drew in her breath, most likely from the brazen lie her former captor pronounced. The three of us froze, fearing those in the other room had heard her. Mr. Green, to his credit, was able to distract them with a cough of his own.

"I can see that," he continued. "If you do not want to part with this piece, perhaps I can arrange for a jeweler to join us, say tomorrow? I would be interested in the whole set, if you could bring them then."

"I believe that can be arranged," said Peters.

A rustling suggested the man and his "daughter" were re-wrapping the jewelry for transport. When things were quiet again, he asked, "Might I suggest we retire to the restaurant below for a meal?"

The Lady Frances shook her head violently, perhaps out of fear that Green's manners might not withstand the scrutiny. Of course, we had no way to signal him to decline. We all held our breath, listening for his response.

"An excellent idea," Green said, with more enthusiasm than a person in his position usually expressed.

The Lady Frances appeared aghast at the prospect of Green making it through an entire meal in his new persona. We could only hope he would be able to continue to deceive the rascals.

After the three left for the restaurant, we followed at a discreet distance and sought some vantage point from which we could observe them without being seen. To do so required both distance and some hotel greenery, making it impossible to follow any conversation. The Lady Frances spent her time chewing on her lower lip to the point I feared she would draw blood. Through her clenched teeth, she mumbled directions to him.

"Take the cup delicately by the handle. That's right. Use that fork for the fish. Dab the mouth, don't swipe...."

"You have done an admirable job, Lady Frances," Holmes said after the waiters took away the first course. "And in only three days. His willingness to take on this task speaks volumes not only of his character, but his devotion to you."

While she didn't take her gaze off her old suitor, I noticed a slight coloring in her cheeks. For the first time, I wondered if Holmes had more than one objective with his current client.

When the waiter rolled out a cart with after-dinner liquors, the woman groaned.

"We haven't had time for more than a cursory discussion of the proper after-meal drinks. Don't order a beer, don't order a beer..."

When Peters' eyes rounded, Green's choice became obvious. To make matters worse, the alcohol forced delicate cracks in his façade. By the time he ordered a second glass, both of his companions were shifting in their chairs and glancing toward the waiter as if to signal the meal was over.

As soon as the waiter appeared, the couple stood, took their leave from Green, and hurried away.

"Quick," said Holmes, "Watson and I will follow them. Lady Frances, please collect Mr. Green and return to our place at Baker Street."

By the time we returned to our flat, Green and the Lady Frances were on opposite sides of the room. The man sat in my chair by the fireplace, his shoulders slumped low. The Lady Frances was enjoying a cup of tea at our small table, her back to the man.

"I have good news," said my friend as he helped himself to his own cup. "We were able to trail the two back to their hotel. Not the best part of the city, but respectable enough I suppose."

"And how is that good news?" asked his client. "Mr. Green most certainly chased them away. They'll not be returning with my jewels for a second meeting."

"But we can be assured they do have the jewels with them. Their discussion with Mr. Green about bringing the rest tomorrow means they most certainly have the whole collection," he said. "Given the type of hotel, I doubt they would trust the staff to keep them in the hotel safe, which means they are most likely in their rooms. The appropriate search should find them. All we need do is wait for them to leave the room."

"And how are we going to get them to do that?"

"I have a plan to draw them out. But we must act quickly. Given Mr. Green's performance at dinner, they may have become suspicious and decide to leave at any moment."

The Lady Frances' gaze slid sideways to study Green, who dutifully sank lower in his chair. "What makes you think we will be able to find my jewels?" she asked.

"I am familiar with the most common places thieves hide such items. Between the two of you, these can be checked in a relatively short period of time. You should be able to recover your missing fortune before they return."

With a sigh, followed by a sip of tea, she nodded. "As long as we don't get caught."

The plan was a rather simple one. Holmes, in the disguise of an elderly rare coin collector would attempt to open their hotel room, appearing to have mistaken it for his own. After showing them the collection in a set of heavy cases, he would convince them to help carry them to the lobby where he was to meet a potential client. The pair would hardly pass up an opportunity to relieve this gentleman of some of his coins for their own gain.

As with Green's deception, Holmes' ruse aroused the interest of Peters and Fraser immediately. They volunteered to help the man with his trip to the lobby and offered to carry his cases for him. Holmes' most brilliant move was to prevent their door from locking, allowing the Lady Frances and Mr. Green quick access.

My role was to remain in the hallway and signal when the three re-appeared. So great was the responsibility I bore—to ensure no one was caught in the deception—my heart thrummed in my chest. I feared its beat was loud enough for all the guests to hear—not to mention almost drowning out the sound of any footsteps on the stairs.

Too soon, I heard voices drifting up the stairwell.

"I must say," Holmes said in his elderly collector's voice, "I don't under-stand my confusion. How could I have mistaken the day I was to meet with the gentleman?"

"It happens," said Peters.

With no hint of annoyance in his voice, I decided he and his accomplice must have relieved Holmes of some of the coins he carried. I didn't hear any more of the conversation because I was already down the hall and knocking on the door to signal the culprits' return.

A crash on the stairs suggested at least a few of the cases had made their way out of Holmes' arms and down the steps. The tinkling that followed signaled that some of the coins had also escaped the cases, providing yet another chance for Peters and Fraser to pocket one or more of the coins. Holmes was obviously hoping to buy us a few more precious seconds to make our own escape. I heard more clatter and some frus-trated sighs drifting up the stairwell, indicating he continued to have problems with the collection.

The Lady Frances and Mr. Green slipped out of the room. The bag they had brought to secrete the recovered jewels hung limply in the Lady Frances' hand. It was obvious they hadn't found her inheritance, but I had no time to ask them about the search. We barely made it to the servants' stairs at the end of the hall.

"Thank you so much for your help," Holmes said, his voice now echoing down the corridor.

He got a pleasant farewell in response (most likely due to the coins now in their possession) before the door to their room shut behind them.

When my friend joined us in the stairwell, he straightened himself and spoke in his usual voice to his clients. "Any luck?"

They shook their heads slowly. "We checked all the places you suggested."

"Let us retire to Baker Street and consider our next move, which must occur quickly. They mentioned leaving tomorrow. Perhaps now is the time to alert Inspector Lestrade of their presence."

"What about my second appointment with them?" Green asked.

"Isn't it obvious?" the Lady Frances asked. "They are no longer interested in selling to you. Your behavior at the restaurant made them suspicious."

"How many times must I apologize? No one told me it was the wrong after-dinner drink."

"An oversight on our part," Holmes said. "We must review our options to see how we might still identify where they have hidden the jewels."

Once outside the hotel, Holmes hailed a cab. As we turned the corner, Mr. Green suddenly ordered the cab to stop.

"What are you doing? Where are you going?" the Lady Frances asked in a shrill voice when he stepped onto the pavement.

"We've tried your methods, Mr. Holmes," he said. "I think it's time to try another."

Our client, wide-eyed with panic, stared first at me and then my friend. "Stop him before he does something foolish."

Holmes held open the door to address the man. "I would suggest you reconsider this tactic. These are desperate people who have shown no mercy in the past. Not to mention any number of legal ramifications for you. If you were to confront them physically—"

"I'll take my chances," he said and closed the door.

"Are you just going to let him go?" the Lady Frances asked. "What if he gets hurt?"

Holmes glanced at me, and I shrugged. While I had no desire to get into a physical altercation, we certainly had the numerical advantage. He sighed and glanced down at his old coin collector's disguise. "I suppose the outfit might add some advantage should we need to confront them. As long as hotel security doesn't become involved..."

By the time the cab was able to turn around and pull up to the hotel, Mr. Green was nowhere to be seen. We immediately moved up the stairs to Peters' room. To our dismay, the door was slightly ajar, but no sounds came through the opening. Holmes put his finger to his lips to warn us to remain silent as he pushed the door wide enough for us to enter.

The two thieves cowered in a corner with Mr. Green standing menacingly over them. Peters' mouth was already swelling, and Miss Fraser had wedged herself between him and the wall. When she heard us enter, she whimpered something about mercy.

Her remark called Peters' and Green's attention to our presence.

"Mr. Holmes, so glad you joined me," Green said. "This man was about to tell me where we can find the jewels, but I had no way to get them without allowing these crooks to possibly slip away. Again."

"And where would the hiding place be?" Holmes asked.

The Australian raised a shaking finger toward a set of valises on a stand near the bed. "The big one. It has a false bottom. You'll find them there."

The Lady Frances rushed to the indicated bag, and I followed to assist her in retrieving her inheritance. She gasped as the bottom was removed and her jewelry revealed.

She spun about to the four behind us. "It's all here."

In several swift moves, she deposited them in the bag she had brought with her earlier.

"Now, Lady Frances," Holmes said, "if you would be so kind as to return to the lobby and request a police officer. I'm certain Scotland Yard would be glad to relieve Mr. Green of his prisoners."

Once Inspector Lestrade and his officers had escorted the culprits from the hotel, the Lady Frances stepped toward Mr. Green, and with an almost timid gaze, smiled at the man. "Thank you, Philip. You were able to retrieve that which even the great Sherlock Holmes could not."

Her former suitor's face flushed, whether from the compliment she paid to his effort or to her use of his given name, I couldn't be certain.

"Lady Frances," Mr. Green said, raising her hand to his lips, "I would have gone through the fires of Hephaestus to return them to you."

"I believe you would," she said, meeting his gaze.

I opened my mouth to protest her dismissal of Holmes' efforts, but he shook his head to stop me. A slight twitch in his lips suggested he wasn't displeased with the result, despite the misplaced credit.

***

Having finally brought full justice to the Lady Frances, Holmes and I celebrated the next evening with an excellent claret with our dinner.

I raised my glass to him. "I have to say, you were very generous in letting Green take the credit for the return of the Lady Frances' jewels."

"My dear Watson, I didn't *let* him claim the victory. It was my intention all along for him to retrieve the jewels, and with it the heart of the woman." After taking a sip from his own glass, he broke into a smile. "I could have easily fooled the thieves with my own disguise as the gem collector. After all, they never questioned me as the coin enthusiast. You also know my present caseload wasn't overly demanding. But the bit of incompetence on my part made Green shine all the brighter, don't you think?"

I stared at him. Did he mean what I thought?

"You know my concern about an unmarried woman of means and her vulnerability to the unscrupulous. I considered it mandatory to attach her to an appropriate companion and protector. And who better than the Hon. Philip Green. I used your own romance with Miss Mary Marston as a basis for developing this attraction between the two."

"I hardly believe you can equate—"

He raised his hand to still my protest. "While I solved the case of the sign of the four, you fell in love with Miss Marston, and she reciprocated. By employing Mr. Green and the Lady Frances as our assistants in this case, I deduced a similar mutual interest should develop between them. To increase the probabilities of success, I manipulated the situation—the flowers were selected for their aphrodisiacal properties, seating them next to each other on the couch to create greater proximity, refining Green's manners."

While I had grown accustomed to my friend's rather brusque observations and theories, in referencing my own courtship, he had gone too far. To say that my love and admiration for the lovely creature who became my wife was due simply to solving the theft of the Agra treasure completely dismissed the deep feelings shared between us. My cheeks grew hot the more I reflected on his observation.

"Now see here, Holmes, I resent your suggestion that Mary and I only wed because of that case."

"It is *only* because of the case you met and wed. This city is teeming with single women. You would not have met her without her seeking out my help to determine the origin of the pearls she'd been receiving. You can't deny that fact."

This comment silenced the next retort on my tongue. I couldn't disagree with that point. The possibility that we would have met otherwise was quite remote. At the same time...

"There have been other single women who have passed through these doors and whose cases we have addressed, and I haven't married them."

"Really, I didn't say it was the only factor. We already knew that Green was devoted to the Lady Frances, but she held some deep-seated abhorrence to the man's comportment. Hence, the pretense of refining his manners. But the true shift in her attitude came from allowing him to be the hero in the recovery of her jewels. Here again, I took a page from your rapid courtship of Miss Marston. Her first words of gratitude were to you, not me. Don't protest, I know you corrected her, but all the same, it was your close encounter with a poisonous dart that caused her to pale."

His rather clinical description of the moment I knew Mary held feelings similar to mine renewed the heartache of my loss.

Oblivious to my pain, he continued. "I deduced Green's heroics were bound to have a similar effect on the Lady Frances. Her concern over his safety when he returned to the hotel and his display of masculine prowess when he confronted the thieves most certainly transformed her opinion of him. The result should be a productive future together for them both."

"If I'm not mistaken," he said, cocking his head to one side, "We are about to confirm whether my conclusions are correct."

Before we could set our glasses onto the table, Mrs. Hudson escorted the Lady Frances and Mr. Green into our rooms.

"I'm terribly sorry to disturb your repast, but we simply couldn't wait to share our news," the Lady Frances said.

After glancing in Holmes' direction, I said, "Let me guess. You are here to announce your impending nuptials."

Despite her upbringing, the woman's mouth dropped open in sheer amazement. "Nuptials?" She glanced at Green, whose face now carried a wooden expression that suggested he didn't share the same shocked opinion of such a future prospect. "Well, I suppose—I mean I am fond—"

"We're going into business together," Green said, his voice as wooden as his expression. "We're becoming detectives."

"Yes. After working with the two of you, we feel we've learned enough about how to deal with criminals that we will be able to do it ourselves," the Lady Frances said, her excitement returning.

"Don't you worry, though," Green said. "We plan to work in South Africa."

Holmes raised his glass, "I pity the lawbreakers there. I'm sure you'll be a formidable opponent. I wish you all the luck."

After toasting to their future endeavors and bidding them farewell, Holmes sank into his chair by the fire and studied the flames there. More to himself than to me, he mumbled, "I was so certain my deductions..."

"Come now, there was no way you could have foreseen this course of events."

"I return to my earlier observation about love. It is emotional and opposed to cold reason, which I value above all. In the future I shall keep to my study of the criminal element where my skills are well-honed and logic prevails. As for the realm of sentiments and passions, I'll leave those to the magpies in the agony columns."

In "The Final Problem," published in 1893, Sherlock Holmes plunges to his death over the Reichenbach Falls in Switzerland after struggling with Professor Moriarty - his archenemy. To Watson's great astonishment, he returns after a three-year mysterious hiatus to resume his practice. "The Adventure of the Empty House" was published in 1903 to the public's delight. Another thirty-four cases followed. It is provided here as background for "The Curious Incident of the Howling Dog on Baker Street."

THE ADVENTURE OF THE EMPTY HOUSE

BY SIR ARTHUR CONAN DOYLE

It was in the spring of the year 1894 that all London was interested, and the fashionable world dismayed, by the murder of the Honourable Ronald Adair under most unusual and inexplicable circumstances. The public has already learned those particulars of the crime which came out in the police investigation; but a good deal was suppressed upon that occasion, since the case for the prosecution was so overwhelmingly strong that it was not necessary to bring forward all the facts. Only now, at the end of nearly ten years, am I allowed to supply those missing links which make up the whole of that remarkable chain. The crime was of interest in itself, but that interest was as nothing to me compared to the inconceivable sequel, which afforded me the greatest shock and surprise of any event in my adventurous life. Even now, after this long interval, I find myself thrilling as I think of it, and feeling once more that sudden flood of joy, amazement, and incredulity which utterly submerged my mind. Let me say to that public which has shown some interest in those glimpses which I have occasionally given them of the thoughts and actions of a very remarkable man that they are not to blame me if I have not shared my knowledge with them, for I should have considered it my first duty to have done so had I not been barred by a positive prohibition from his own lips, which was only withdrawn upon the third of last month.

It can be imagined that my close intimacy with Sherlock Holmes had interested me deeply in crime, and that after his disappearance I never failed to read with care the various problems which came before the public, and I even attempted more than once for my own private satisfaction to employ his methods in their solution, though with indifferent success. There was none, however, which appealed to me like this tragedy of Ronald Adair. As I read the evidence at the inquest, which led up to a verdict of wilful murder against some person or persons unknown, I realized more clearly than I had ever done the loss which the community had sustained by the death of Sherlock Holmes. There were points about this strange business which would, I was sure, have specially appealed to him, and the efforts of the police would have been supplemented, or more probably anticipated, by the trained observation and the alert mind of the first criminal agent in Europe. All day as I drove upon my round I turned over the case in my mind, and found no explanation which appeared to me to be adequate. At the risk of telling a twice-told tale I will recapitulate the facts as they were known to the public at the conclusion of the inquest.

The Honourable Ronald Adair was the second son of the Earl of Maynooth, at that time Governor of one of the Australian Colonies. Adair's mother had returned from Australia to undergo the operation for cataract, and she, her son Ronald, and her daughter Hilda were living together at 427, Park Lane. The youth moved in the best society, had, so far as was known, no enemies, and no particular vices. He had been engaged to Miss Edith Woodley, of Carstairs, but the engagement had been broken off by mutual consent some months before, and there was no sign that it had left any very profound feeling behind it. For the rest the man's life moved in a narrow and conventional circle, for his habits were quiet and his nature unemotional. Yet it was upon this easy-going young aristocrat that death came in most strange and unexpected form between the hours of ten and eleven-twenty on the night of March 30, 1894.

Ronald Adair was fond of cards, playing continually, but never for such stakes as would hurt him. He was a member of the Baldwin, the

Cavendish, and the Bagatelle card clubs. It was shown that after dinner on the day of his death he had played a rubber of whist at the latter club. He had also played there in the afternoon. The evidence of those who had played with him—Mr. Murray, Sir John Hardy, and Colonel Moran— showed that the game was whist, and that there was a fairly equal fall of the cards. Adair might have lost five pounds, but not more. His fortune was a considerable one, and such a loss could not in any way affect him. He had played nearly every day at one club or other, but he was a cautious player, and usually rose a winner. It came out in evidence that in partner- ship with Colonel Moran he had actually won as much as four hundred and twenty pounds in a sitting some weeks before from Godfrey Milner and Lord Balmoral. So much for his recent history, as it came out at the inquest.

On the evening of the crime he returned from the club exactly at ten. His mother and sister were out spending the evening with a relation. The servant deposed that she heard him enter the front room on the second floor, generally used as his sitting-room. She had lit a fire there, and as it smoked she had opened the window. No sound was heard from the room until eleven-twenty, the hour of the return of Lady Maynooth and her daughter. Desiring to say good-night, she had attempted to enter her son's room. The door was locked on the inside, and no answer could be got to their cries and knocking. Help was obtained and the door forced. The unfortunate young man was found lying near the table. His head had been horribly mutilated by an expanding revolver bullet, but no weapon of any sort was to be found in the room. On the table lay two bank-notes for ten pounds each and seventeen pounds ten in silver and gold, the money arranged in little piles of varying amount. There were some figures also upon a sheet of paper with the names of some club friends opposite to them, from which it was conjectured that before his death he was endeav- ouring to make out his losses or winnings at cards.

A minute examination of the circumstances served only to make the case more complex. In the first place, no reason could be given why the young man should have fastened the door upon the inside. There was the possibility that the murderer had done this and had afterwards escaped by the window. The drop was at least twenty feet, however, and a bed of crocuses in full bloom lay beneath. Neither the flowers nor the earth showed any sign of having been disturbed, nor were there any marks upon the narrow strip of grass which separated the house from the road. Apparently, therefore, it was the young man himself who had fastened the door. But how did he come by his death? No one could have climbed up to the window without leaving traces. Suppose a man had fired through the window, it would indeed be a remarkable shot who could with a revolver inflict so deadly a wound. Again, Park Lane is a frequented thoroughfare, and there is a cab-stand within a hundred yards of the house. No one had heard a shot. And yet there was the dead man, and there the revolver bullet, which had mushroomed out, as soft-nosed bullets will, and so inflicted a wound which must have caused instantaneous death. Such were the circumstances of the Park Lane Mystery, which were further complicated by entire absence of motive, since, as I have said, young Adair was not known to have any enemy, and no attempt had been made to remove the money or valuables in the room.

All day I turned these facts over in my mind, endeavouring to hit upon some theory which could reconcile them all, and to find that line of least resistance which my poor friend had declared to be the starting-point of every investigation. I confess that I made little progress. In the evening I strolled across the Park, and found myself about six o'clock at the Oxford Street end of Park Lane. A group of loafers upon the pavements, all staring up at a particular window, directed me to the house which I had come to see. A tall, thin man with coloured glasses, whom I strongly suspected of being a plain-clothes detective, was pointing out some theory of his own, while the others crowded round to listen to what he said. I got as near him as I could, but his observations seemed to me to be absurd, so I withdrew again in some disgust. As I did so I struck against an elderly deformed man, who had been behind me, and I knocked down several books which he was carrying. I remember that as I picked them up I observed the title of one of them, "The Origin of Tree Worship," and it struck me that the fellow must be some poor bibliophile who, either as a trade or as a hobby, was a collector of obscure volumes. I endeavoured to apologize for the accident, but it was evident that these books which I had so unfortunately maltreated were very precious objects in the eyes of their owner. With a snarl of contempt he turned upon his heel, and I saw his curved back and white side-whiskers disappear among the throng.

My observations of No. 427, Park Lane did little to clear up the problem in which I was interested. The house was separated from the street by a low wall and railing, the whole not more than five feet high. It was perfectly easy, therefore, for anyone to get into the garden, but the window was entirely inaccessible, since there was no water-pipe or anything which could help the most active man to climb it. More puzzled than ever, I retraced my steps to Kensington. I had not been in my study five minutes when the maid entered to say that a person desired to see me. To my astonishment it was none other than my strange old book-collector, his sharp, wizened face peering out from a frame of white hair, and his precious volumes, a dozen of them at least, wedged under his right arm.

"You're surprised to see me, sir," said he, in a strange, croaking voice.

I acknowledged that I was.

"Well, I've a conscience, sir, and when I chanced to see you go into this house, as I came hobbling after you, I thought to myself, I'll just step in and see that kind gentleman, and tell him that if I was a bit gruff in my manner there was not any harm meant, and that I am much obliged to him for picking up my books."

"You make too much of a trifle," said I. "May I ask how you knew who I was?"

"Well, sir, if it isn't too great a liberty, I am a neighbour of yours, for you'll find my little bookshop at the corner of Church Street, and very happy to see you, I am sure. Maybe you collect yourself, sir; here's 'British Birds,' and 'Catullus,' and 'The Holy War'—a bargain every one of them. With five volumes you could just fill that gap on that second shelf. It looks untidy, does it not, sir?"

I moved my head to look at the cabinet behind me. When I turned again Sherlock Holmes was standing smiling at me across my study table. I rose to my feet, stared at him for some seconds in utter amazement, and then it appears that I must have fainted for the first and the last time in my life. Certainly a grey mist swirled before my eyes, and when it cleared

I found my collar-ends undone and the tingling after-taste of brandy upon my lips. Holmes was bending over my chair, his flask in his hand.

"My dear Watson," said the well-remembered voice, "I owe you a thousand apologies. I had no idea that you would be so affected."

I gripped him by the arm.

"Holmes!" I cried. "Is it really you? Can it indeed be that you are alive? Is it possible that you succeeded in climbing out of that awful abyss?"

"Wait a moment," said he. "Are you sure that you are really fit to discuss things? I have given you a serious shock by my unnecessarily dramatic reappearance."

"I am all right, but indeed, Holmes, I can hardly believe my eyes. Good heavens, to think that you—you of all men—should be standing in my study!" Again I gripped him by the sleeve and felt the thin, sinewy arm beneath it. "Well, you're not a spirit, anyhow," said I. "My dear chap, I am overjoyed to see you. Sit down and tell me how you came alive out of that dreadful chasm."

He sat opposite to me and lit a cigarette in his old nonchalant manner. He was dressed in the seedy frock- coat of the book merchant, but the rest of that individual lay in a pile of white hair and old books upon the table. Holmes looked even thinner and keener than of old, but there was a dead-white tinge in his aquiline face which told me that his life recently had not been a healthy one.

"I am glad to stretch myself, Watson," said he. "It is no joke when a tall man has to take a foot off his stature for several hours on end. Now, my dear fellow, in the matter of these explanations we have, if I may ask for your co-operation, a hard and dangerous night's work in front of us. Perhaps it would be better if I gave you an account of the whole situation when that work is finished."

"I am full of curiosity. I should much prefer to hear now." "You'll come with me to-night?"

"When you like and where you like."

"This is indeed like the old days. We shall have time for a mouthful of dinner before we need go. Well, then, about that chasm. I had no serious difficulty in getting out of it, for the very simple reason that I never was in it."

"You never were in it?"

"No, Watson, I never was in it. My note to you was absolutely genuine. I had little doubt that I had come to the end of my career when I perceived the somewhat sinister figure of the late Professor Moriarty standing upon the narrow pathway which led to safety. I read an inexorable purpose in his grey eyes. I exchanged some remarks with him, therefore, and obtained his courteous permission to write the short note which you afterwards received. I left it with my cigarette-box and my stick and I walked along the pathway, Moriarty still at my heels. When I reached the end I stood at bay. He drew no weapon, but he rushed at me and threw his long arms around me. He knew that his own game was up, and was only anxious to revenge himself upon me. We tottered together upon the brink of the fall. I have some knowledge, however, of baritsu, or the Japanese system of wrestling, which has more than once been very useful to me. I slipped through his grip, and he with a horrible scream kicked madly for a few seconds and clawed the air with both his hands. But for all his efforts he could not get his balance, and over he went. With my face over the brink I saw him fall for a long way. Then he struck a rock, bounded off, and splashed into the water."

I listened with amazement to this explanation, which Holmes delivered between the puffs of his cigarette.

"But the tracks!" I cried. "I saw with my own eyes that two went down the path and none returned."

"It came about in this way. The instant that the Professor had disappeared it struck me what a really extraordinarily lucky chance Fate had placed in my way. I knew that Moriarty was not the only man who had sworn my death. There were at least three others whose desire for vengeance upon me would only be increased by the death of their leader. They were all most dangerous men. One or other would certainly get me. On the other hand, if all the world was convinced that I was dead they would take liberties, these men, they would lay themselves open, and sooner or later I could destroy them. Then it would be time for me to announce that I was still in the land of the living. So rapidly does the brain act that I believe I had thought this all out before Professor Moriarty had reached the bottom of the Reichenbach Fall.

"I stood up and examined the rocky wall behind me. In your picturesque account of the matter, which I read with great interest some months later, you assert that the wall was sheer. This was not literally true. A few small footholds presented themselves, and there was some indication of a ledge. The cliff is so high that to climb it all was an obvious impossibility, and it was equally impossible to make my way along the wet path without leaving some tracks. I might, it is true, have reversed my boots, as I have done on similar occasions, but the sight of three sets of tracks in one direction would certainly have suggested a deception. On the whole, then, it was best that I should risk the climb. It was not a pleasant business, Watson. The fall roared beneath me. I am not a fanciful person, but I give you my word that I seemed to hear Moriarty's voice screaming at me out of the abyss. A mistake would have been fatal. More than once, as tufts of grass came out in my hand or my foot slipped in the wet notches of the rock, I thought that I was gone. But I struggled upwards, and at last I reached a ledge several feet deep and covered with soft green moss, where I could lie unseen in the most perfect comfort. There I was stretched when you, my dear Watson, and all your following were investigating in the most sympathetic and inefficient manner the circumstances of my death.

"At last, when you had all formed your inevitable and totally erroneous conclusions, you departed for the hotel and I was left alone. I had imagined that I had reached the end of my adventures, but a very unexpected occurrence showed me that there were surprises still in store for me. A huge rock, falling from above, boomed past me, struck the path, and bounded over into the chasm. For an instant I thought that it was an accident; but a moment later, looking up, I saw a man's head against the darkening sky, and another stone struck the very ledge upon which I was stretched, within a foot of my head. Of course, the meaning of this was obvious. Moriarty had not been alone. A confederate—and even that one glance had told me how dangerous a man that confederate was—had kept guard while the Professor had attacked me. From a distance, unseen by me, he had been a witness of his friend's death and of my escape. He had waited, and then, making his way round to the top of the cliff, he had endeavoured to succeed where his comrade had failed.

"I did not take long to think about it, Watson. Again I saw that grim face look over the cliff, and I knew that it was the precursor of another stone. I scrambled down on to the path. I don't think I could have done it in cold blood. It was a hundred times more difficult than getting up. But I had no time to think of the danger, for another stone sang past me as I hung by my hands from the edge of the ledge. Halfway down I slipped, but by the blessing of God I landed, torn and bleeding, upon the path. I took to my heels, did ten miles over the mountains in the darkness, and a week later I found myself in Florence with the certainty that no one in the world knew what had become of me.

"I had only one confidant—my brother Mycroft. I owe you many apologies, my dear Watson, but it was all- important that it should be thought I was dead, and it is quite certain that you would not have written so convincing an account of my unhappy end had you not yourself thought that it was true. Several times during the last three years I have taken up my pen to write to you, but always I feared lest your affectionate regard for me should tempt you to some indiscretion which would betray my secret. For that reason I turned away from you this evening when you upset my books, for I was in danger at the time, and any show of surprise and emotion upon your part might have drawn attention to my identity and led to the most deplorable and irreparable results. As to Mycroft, I had to confide in him in order to obtain the money which I needed. The course of events in London did not run so well as I had hoped, for the trial of the Moriarty gang left two of its most dangerous members, my own most vindictive enemies, at liberty. I travelled for two years in Tibet, therefore, and amused myself by visiting Lhassa and spending some days with the head Llama. You may have read of the remarkable explorations of a Norwegian named Sigerson, but I am sure that it never occurred to you that you were receiving news of your friend. I then passed through Persia, looked in at Mecca, and paid a short but interesting visit to the Khalifa at Khartoum, the results of which I have communicated to the Foreign Office. Returning to France I spent some months in a research into the coal-tar derivatives, which I conducted in a laboratory at Mont-pelier, in the South of France. Having concluded this to my satisfaction, and learning that only one of my enemies was now left in London, I was about to return when my movements were hastened by the news of this very remarkable Park Lane Mystery, which not only appealed to me by its own merits, but which seemed to offer some most peculiar personal opportunities. I came over at once to London, called in my own person at Baker Street, threw Mrs. Hudson into violent hysterics, and found that Mycroft had preserved my rooms and my papers exactly as they had always been. So it was, my dear Watson, that at two o'clock to-day I found myself in my old arm-chair in my own old room, and only wishing that I could have seen my old friend Watson in the other chair which he has so often adorned."

Such was the remarkable narrative to which I listened on that April evening—a narrative which would have been utterly incredible to me had it not been confirmed by the actual sight of the tall, spare figure and the keen, eager face, which I had never thought to see again. In some manner he had learned of my own sad bereavement, and his sympathy was shown in his manner rather than in his words. "Work is the best antidote to sorrow, my dear Watson," said he, "and I have a piece of work for us both to-night which, if we can bring it to a successful conclusion, will in itself justify a man's life on this planet." In vain I begged him to tell me more. "You will hear and see enough before morning," he answered. "We have three years of the past to discuss. Let that suffice until half-past nine, when we start upon the notable adventure of the empty house."

It was indeed like old times when, at that hour, I found myself seated beside him in a hansom, my revolver in my pocket and the thrill of adventure in my heart. Holmes was cold and stern and silent. As the gleam of the street-lamps flashed upon his austere features I saw that his brows were drawn down in thought and his thin lips compressed. I knew not what wild beast we were about to hunt down in the dark jungle of criminal London, but I was well assured from the bearing of this master huntsman that the adventure was a most grave one, while the sardonic smile which occasionally broke through his ascetic gloom boded little good for the object of our quest.

I had imagined that we were bound for Baker Street, but Holmes stopped the cab at the corner of Cavendish Square. I observed that as he stepped out he gave a most searching glance to right and left, and at every subsequent street corner he took the utmost pains to assure that he was not followed. Our route was certainly a singular one. Holmes's knowledge of the byways of London was extraordinary, and on this occasion he passed rapidly, and with an assured step, through a network of mews and stables the very existence of which I had never known. We emerged at last into a small road, lined with old, gloomy houses, which led us into Manchester Street, and so to Blandford Street. Here he turned swiftly down a narrow passage, passed through a wooden gate into a deserted yard, and then opened with a key the back door of a house. We entered together and he closed it behind us.

The place was pitch-dark, but it was evident to me that it was an empty house. Our feet creaked and crackled over the bare planking, and my outstretched hand touched a wall from which the paper was hanging in ribbons. Holmes's cold, thin fingers closed round my wrist and led me forwards down a long hall, until I dimly saw the murky fanlight over the door. Here Holmes turned suddenly to the right, and we found ourselves in a large, square, empty room, heavily shadowed in the corners, but faintly lit in the centre from the lights of the street beyond. There was no lamp near and the window was thick with dust, so that we could only just discern each other's figures within. My companion put his hand upon my shoulder and his lips close to my ear.

"Do you know where we are?" he whispered.

"Surely that is Baker Street," I answered, staring through the dim window.

"Exactly. We are in Camden House, which stands opposite to our own old quarters." "But why are we here?"

"Because it commands so excellent a view of that picturesque pile. Might I trouble you, my dear Watson, to draw a little nearer to the window, taking every precaution not to show yourself, and then to look up at our old rooms—the starting-point of so many of our little adventures? We will see if my three years of absence have entirely taken away my power to surprise you."

I crept forward and looked across at the familiar window. As my eyes fell upon it I gave a gasp and a cry of amazement. The blind was down and a strong light was burning in the room. The shadow of a man who was seated in a chair within was thrown in hard, black outline upon the luminous screen of the window. There was no mistaking the poise of the head, the squareness of the shoulders, the sharpness of the features. The face was turned half-round, and the effect was that of one of those black silhouettes which our grandparents loved to frame. It was a perfect reproduction of Holmes. So amazed was I that I threw out my hand to make sure that the man himself was standing beside me. He was quivering with silent laughter.

"Well?" said he.

"Good heavens!" I cried. "It is marvellous."

"I trust that age doth not wither nor custom stale my infinite variety," said he, and I recognised in his voice the joy and pride which the artist takes in his own creation. "It really is rather like me, is it not?"

"I should be prepared to swear that it was you."

"The credit of the execution is due to Monsieur Oscar Meunier, of Grenoble, who spent some days in doing the moulding. It is a bust in wax. The rest I arranged myself during my visit to Baker Street this afternoon."

"But why?"

"Because, my dear Watson, I had the strongest possible reason for wishing certain people to think that I was there when I was really elsewhere."

"And you thought the rooms were watched?"

"I *knew* that they were watched."

"By whom?"

"By my old enemies, Watson. By the charming society whose leader lies in the Reichenbach Fall. You must remember that they knew, and only they knew, that I was still alive. Sooner or later they believed that I should come back to my rooms. They watched them continuously, and this morning they saw me arrive."

"How do you know?"

"Because I recognised their sentinel when I glanced out of my window. He is a harmless enough fellow, Parker by name, a garroter by trade, and a remarkable performer upon the Jew's harp. I cared nothing for him. But I cared a great deal for the much more formidable person who was behind him, the bosom friend of Moriarty, the man who dropped the rocks over the cliff, the most cunning and dangerous criminal in London. That is the man who is after me to-night, Watson, and that is the man who is quite unaware that we are after HIM."

My friend's plans were gradually revealing themselves. From this convenient retreat the watchers were being watched and the trackers tracked. That angular shadow up yonder was the bait and we were the hunters. In silence we stood together in the darkness and watched the hurrying figures who passed and repassed in front of us. Holmes was silent and motionless; but I could tell that he was keenly alert, and that his eyes were fixed intently upon the stream of passers-by. It was a bleak and boisterous night, and the wind whistled shrilly down the long street. Many people were moving to and fro, most of them muffled in their coats and cravats. Once or twice it seemed to me that I had seen the same figure before, and I especially noticed two men who appeared to be sheltering themselves from the wind in the doorway of a house some distance up the street. I tried to draw my companion's attention to them, but he gave a little ejaculation of impatience and continued to stare into the street. More than once he fidgeted with his feet and tapped rapidly with his fingers upon the wall. It was evident to me that he was becoming uneasy and that his plans were not working out altogether as he had hoped. At last, as midnight approached and the street gradually cleared, he paced up and down the room in uncontrollable agitation. I was about to make some remark to him when I raised my eyes to the lighted window and again experienced almost as great a surprise as before. I clutched Holmes's arm and pointed upwards.

"The shadow has moved!" I cried.

It was, indeed, no longer the profile, but the back, which was turned towards us.

Three years had certainly not smoothed the asperities of his temper or his impatience with a less active intelligence than his own.

"Of course it has moved," said he. "Am I such a farcical bungler, Watson, that I should erect an obvious dummy and expect that some of the sharpest men in Europe would be deceived by it? We have been in this room two hours, and Mrs. Hudson has made some change in that figure eight times, or once in every quarter of an hour. She works it from the front so that her shadow may never be seen. Ah!" He drew in his breath with a shrill, excited intake. In the dim light I saw his head thrown forward, his whole attitude rigid with attention. Outside, the street was absolutely deserted. Those two men might still be crouching in the door-way, but I could no longer see them. All was still and dark, save only that brilliant yellow screen in front of us with the black figure outlined upon its centre. Again in the utter silence I heard that thin, sibilant note which spoke of intense suppressed excitement. An instant later he pulled me back into the blackest corner of the room, and I felt his warning hand upon my lips. The fingers which clutched me were quivering. Never had I known my friend more moved, and yet the dark street still stretched lonely and motionless before us.

But suddenly I was aware of that which his keener senses had already distinguished. A low, stealthy sound came to my ears, not from the direc-tion of Baker Street, but from the back of the very house in which we lay concealed. A door opened and shut. An instant later steps crept down the passage—steps which were meant to be silent, but which reverberated harshly through the empty house. Holmes crouched back against the wall and I did the same, my hand closing upon the handle of my revolver. Peering through the gloom, I saw the vague outline of a man, a shade blacker than the blackness of the open door. He stood for an instant, and then he crept forward, crouching, menacing, into the room. He was within three yards of us, this sinister figure, and I had braced myself to meet his spring, before I realized that he had no idea of our presence. He passed close beside us, stole over to the window, and very softly and noiselessly raised it for half a foot. As he sank to the level of this opening the light of the street, no longer dimmed by the dusty glass, fell full upon his face. The man seemed to be beside himself with excitement. His two eyes shone like stars and his features were working convulsively. He was an elderly man, with a thin, projecting nose, a high, bald forehead, and a huge grizzled moustache. An opera-hat was pushed to the back of his head, and an evening dress shirt-front gleamed out through his open overcoat. His face was gaunt and swarthy, scored with deep, savage lines. In his hand he carried what appeared to be a stick, but as he laid it down upon the floor it gave a metallic clang. Then from the pocket of his overcoat he drew a bulky object, and he busied himself in some task which ended with a loud, sharp click, as if a spring or bolt had fallen into its place. Still kneeling upon the floor he bent forward and threw all his weight and strength upon some lever, with the result that there came a long, whirling, grinding noise, ending once more in a powerful click. He straightened himself then, and I saw that what he held in his hand was a sort of gun, with a curiously misshapen butt. He opened it at the breech, put something in, and snapped the breech-block. Then, crouching down, he rested the end of the barrel upon the ledge of the open window, and I saw his long moustache droop over the stock and his eye gleam as it peered along the sights. I heard a little sigh of satisfaction as he cuddled the butt into his shoulder, and saw that amazing target, the black man on the yellow ground, standing clear at the end of his fore sight. For an instant he was rigid and motionless. Then his finger tightened on the trigger. There was a strange, loud whiz and a long, silvery tinkle of broken glass. At that instant Holmes sprang like a tiger on to the marksman's back and hurled him flat upon his face. He was up again in a moment, and with convulsive strength he seized Holmes by the throat; but I struck him on the head with the butt of my revolver and he dropped again upon the floor. I fell upon him, and as I held him my comrade blew a shrill call upon a whistle. There was the clatter of running feet upon the pavement, and two policemen in uniform, with one plain-clothes detective, rushed through the front entrance and into the room.

"That you, Lestrade?" said Holmes.

"Yes, Mr. Holmes. I took the job myself. It's good to see you back in London, sir."

"I think you want a little unofficial help. Three undetected murders in one year won't do, Lestrade. But you handled the Molesey Mystery with less than your usual—that's to say, you handled it fairly well."

We had all risen to our feet, our prisoner breathing hard, with a stalwart constable on each side of him. Already a few loiterers had begun to collect in the street. Holmes stepped up to the window, closed it, and dropped the blinds. Lestrade had produced two candles and the policemen had uncovered their lanterns. I was able at last to have a good look at our prisoner.

It was a tremendously virile and yet sinister face which was turned towards us. With the brow of a philosopher above and the jaw of a sensualist below, the man must have started with great capacities for good or for evil. But one could not look upon his cruel blue eyes, with their drooping, cynical lids, or upon the fierce, aggressive nose and the threatening, deep-lined brow, without reading Nature's plainest danger- signals. He took no heed of any of us, but his eyes were fixed upon Holmes's face with an expression in which hatred and amazement were equally blended. "You fiend!" he kept on muttering. "You clever, clever fiend!"

"Ah, Colonel!" said Holmes, arranging his rumpled collar; "'journeys end in lovers' meetings,' as the old play says. I don't think I have had the pleasure of seeing you since you favoured me with those attentions as I lay on the ledge above the Reichenbach Fall."

The Colonel still stared at my friend like a man in a trance. "You cunning, cunning fiend!" was all that he could say.

"I have not introduced you yet," said Holmes. "This, gentlemen, is Colonel Sebastian Moran, once of Her Majesty's Indian Army, and the best heavy game shot that our Eastern Empire has ever produced. I believe I am correct, Colonel, in saying that your bag of tigers still remains unrivalled?"

The fierce old man said nothing, but still glared at my companion; with his savage eyes and bristling moustache he was wonderfully like a tiger himself.

"I wonder that my very simple stratagem could deceive so old a shikari," said Holmes. "It must be very familiar to you. Have you not tethered a young kid under a tree, lain above it with your rifle, and waited for the bait to bring up your tiger? This empty house is my tree and you are my tiger. You have possibly had other guns in reserve in case there should be several tigers, or in the unlikely supposition of your own aim failing you. These," he pointed around, "are my other guns. The parallel is exact."

Colonel Moran sprang forward, with a snarl of rage, but the constables dragged him back. The fury upon his face was terrible to look at.

"I confess that you had one small surprise for me," said Holmes. "I did not anticipate that you would yourself make use of this empty house and this convenient front window. I had imagined you as operating from the street, where my friend Lestrade and his merry men were awaiting you. With that exception all has gone as I expected."

Colonel Moran turned to the official detective.

"You may or may not have just cause for arresting me," said he, "but at least there can be no reason why I should submit to the gibes of this person. If I am in the hands of the law let things be done in a legal way."

"Well, that's reasonable enough," said Lestrade. "Nothing further you have to say, Mr. Holmes, before we go?"

Holmes had picked up the powerful air-gun from the floor and was examining its mechanism.

"An admirable and unique weapon," said he, "noiseless and of tremendous power. I knew Von Herder, the blind German mechanic, who constructed it to the order of the late Professor Moriarty. For years I have been aware of its existence, though I have never before had the opportunity of handling it. I commend it very specially to your attention, Lestrade, and also the bullets which fit it."

"You can trust us to look after that, Mr. Holmes," said Lestrade, as the whole party moved towards the door. "Anything further to say?"

"Only to ask what charge you intend to prefer?"

"What charge, sir? Why, of course, the attempted murder of Mr. Sherlock Holmes."

"Not so, Lestrade. I do not propose to appear in the matter at all. To you, and to you only, belongs the credit of the remarkable arrest which you have effected. Yes, Lestrade, I congratulate you! With your usual happy mixture of cunning and audacity you have got him."

"Got him! Got whom, Mr. Holmes?"

"The man that the whole force has been seeking in vain—Colonel Sebastian Moran, who shot the Honourable Ronald Adair with an expanding bullet from an air-gun through the open window of the second- floor front of No. 427, Park Lane, upon the 30th of last month. That's the charge, Lestrade. And now, Watson, if you can endure the draught from a broken window, I think that half an hour in my study over a cigar may afford you some profitable amusement."

Our old chambers had been left unchanged through the supervision of Mycroft Holmes and the immediate care of Mrs. Hudson. As I entered I saw, it is true, an unwonted tidiness, but the old landmarks were all in their place. There were the chemical corner and the acid-stained, deal-topped table. There upon a shelf was the row of formidable scrap-books and books of reference which many of our fellow-citizens would have been so glad to burn. The diagrams, the violin-case, and the pipe-rack—even the Persian slipper which contained the tobacco—all met my eyes as I glanced round me. There were two occupants of the room—one Mrs. Hudson, who beamed upon us both as we entered; the other the strange dummy which had played so important a part in the evening's adventures. It was a wax-coloured model of my friend, so admirably done that it was a perfect facsimile. It stood on a small pedestal table with an old dressing-gown of Holmes's so draped round it that the illusion from the street was absolutely perfect.

"I hope you preserved all precautions, Mrs. Hudson?" said Holmes.

"I went to it on my knees, sir, just as you told me."

"Excellent. You carried the thing out very well. Did you observe where the bullet went?"

"Yes, sir. I'm afraid it has spoilt your beautiful bust, for it passed right through the head and flattened itself on the wall. I picked it up from the carpet. Here it is!"

Holmes held it out to me. "A soft revolver bullet, as you perceive, Watson. There's genius in that, for who would expect to find such a thing fired from an air-gun. All right, Mrs. Hudson, I am much obliged for your assistance. And now, Watson, let me see you in your old seat once more, for there are several points which I should like to discuss with you."

He had thrown off the seedy frock-coat, and now he was the Holmes of old in the mouse-coloured dressing- gown which he took from his effigy.

"The old shikari's nerves have not lost their steadiness nor his eyes their keenness," said he, with a laugh, as he inspected the shattered forehead of his bust.

"Plumb in the middle of the back of the head and smack through the brain. He was the best shot in India, and I expect that there are few better in London. Have you heard the name?"

"No, I have not."

"Well, well, such is fame! But, then, if I remember aright, you had not heard the name of Professor James Moriarty, who had one of the great brains of the century. Just give me down my index of biographies from the shelf."

He turned over the pages lazily, leaning back in his chair and blowing great clouds from his cigar.

"My collection of M's is a fine one," said he. "Moriarty himself is enough to make any letter illustrious, and here is Morgan the poisoner, and Merridew of abominable memory, and Mathews, who knocked out my left canine in the waiting-room at Charing Cross, and, finally, here is our friend of to-night."

He handed over the book, and I read: "MORAN, SEBASTIAN, COLONEL. Unemployed. Formerly 1st Bengalore Pioneers. Born London, 1840. Son of Sir Augustus Moran, C.B., once British Minister to Persia. Educated Eton and Oxford. Served in Jowaki Campaign, Afghan Campaign, Charasiab (despatches), Sherpur, and Cabul. Author of 'Heavy Game of the Western Himalayas,' 1881; 'Three Months in the Jungle,' 1884. Address: Conduit Street. Clubs: The Anglo-Indian, the Tankerville, the Bagatelle Card Club."

On the margin was written, in Holmes's precise hand: "The second most dangerous man in London."

"This is astonishing," said I, as I handed back the volume. "The man's career is that of an honourable soldier."

"It is true," Holmes answered. "Up to a certain point he did well. He was always a man of iron nerve, and the story is still told in India how he crawled down a drain after a wounded man-eating tiger. There are some trees, Watson, which grow to a certain height and then suddenly develop some unsightly eccentricity. You will see it often in humans. I have a theory that the individual represents in his development the whole procession of his ancestors, and that such a sudden turn to good or evil stands for some strong influence which came into the line of his pedigree. The person becomes, as it were, the epitome of the history of his own family."

"It is surely rather fanciful."

"Well, I don't insist upon it. Whatever the cause, Colonel Moran began to go wrong. Without any open scandal, he still made India too hot to hold him. He retired, came to London, and again acquired an evil name.

It was at this time that he was sought out by Professor Moriarty, to whom for a time he was chief of the staff. Moriarty supplied him liberally with money and used him only in one or two very high-class jobs which no ordinary criminal could have undertaken. You may have some recollection of the death of Mrs. Stewart, of Lauder, in 1887. Not? Well, I am sure Moran was at the bottom of it; but nothing could be proved. So cleverly was the Colonel concealed that even when the Moriarty gang was broken up we could not incriminate him. You remember at that date, when I called upon you in your rooms, how I put up the shutters for fear of air- guns? No doubt you thought me fanciful. I knew exactly what I was doing, for I knew of the existence of this remarkable gun, and I knew also that one of the best shots in the world would be behind it. When we were in Switzerland he followed us with Moriarty, and it was undoubtedly he who gave me that evil five minutes on the Reichenbach ledge.

"You may think that I read the papers with some attention during my sojourn in France, on the look-out for any chance of laying him by the heels. So long as he was free in London my life would really not have been worth living. Night and day the shadow would have been over me, and sooner or later his chance must have come. What could I do? I could not shoot him at sight, or I should myself be in the dock. There was no use appealing to a magistrate. They cannot interfere on the strength of what would appear to them to be a wild suspicion. So I could do nothing. But I watched the criminal news, knowing that sooner or later I should get him. Then came the death of this Ronald Adair. My chance had come at last! Knowing what I did, was it not certain that Colonel Moran had done it? He had played cards with the lad; he had followed him home from the club; he had shot him through the open window. There was not a doubt of it. The bullets alone are enough to put his head in a noose. I came over at once. I was seen by the sentinel, who would, I knew, direct the Colonel's attention to my presence. He could not fail to connect my sudden return with his crime and to be terribly alarmed. I was sure that he would make an attempt to get me out of the way AT ONCE, and would bring round his murderous weapon for that purpose. I left him an excellent mark in the window, and, having warned the police that they might be needed—by the way, Watson, you spotted their presence in that doorway with unerring accuracy—I took up what seemed to me to be a judicious post for observation, never dreaming that he would choose the same spot for his attack. Now, my dear Watson, does anything remain for me to explain?"

"Yes," said I. "You have not made it clear what was Colonel Moran's motive in murdering the Honourable Ronald Adair."

"Ah! my dear Watson, there we come into those realms of conjecture where the most logical mind may be at fault. Each may form his own hypothesis upon the present evidence, and yours is as likely to be correct as mine."

"You have formed one, then?"

"I think that it is not difficult to explain the facts. It came out in evidence that Colonel Moran and young Adair had between them won a considerable amount of money. Now, Moran undoubtedly played foul—of that I have long been aware. I believe that on the day of the murder Adair had discovered that Moran was cheating. Very likely he had spoken to him privately, and had threatened to expose him unless he voluntarily resigned his membership of the club and promised not to play cards again. It is unlikely that a youngster like Adair would at once make a hideous scandal by exposing a well-known man so much older than himself. Probably he acted as I suggest. The exclusion from his clubs would mean ruin to Moran, who lived by his ill- gotten card gains. He therefore murdered Adair, who at the time was endeavouring to work out how much money he should himself return, since he could not profit by his partner's foul play. He locked the door lest the ladies should surprise him and insist upon knowing what he was doing with these names and coins. Will it pass?"

"I have no doubt that you have hit upon the truth."

"It will be verified or disproved at the trial. Meanwhile, come what may, Colonel Moran will trouble us no more, the famous air-gun of Von Herder will embellish the Scotland Yard Museum, and once again Mr. Sherlock Holmes is free to devote his life to examining those interesting little problems which the complex life of London so plentifully presents."

THE CURIOUS INCIDENT OF THE HOWLING DOG ON BAKER STREET

On a fine spring day in 1894, Ezra raised his head from his pillow at the foot of the couch and glanced up at Cyril. The cat lay half on the sofa and half on the window ledge. Now past its zenith, the sun sent its warm spring rays directly onto the cat's back. The regal tabby's green eyes were mere slits, but Ezra knew they monitored the street scene with unwavering vigilance.

Their mistress' sitting room at 224 Baker Street reflected the woman's elegance and charm, with high ceilings, intricate plasterwork, and tall sash windows. The burgundy velvet couch where Cyril perched complemented the flowered wallpaper. At one time, the room held several round tables exhibiting various antiques, and the two had to tread carefully not to upset anything, but they had all disappeared after her death. Now, few entered this room except for Cyril, the cat, and Ezra, her faithful corgi. Even the master, away on an extended business trip, rarely entered.

The feline widened his eyes and announced to his companion, "The short one is leaving."

The corgi raised his head, lifted his ears, and stilled. "It's the one with the limp. Gives his stride a different rhythm." Another listen. "The one who smokes those French cigarettes is coming back, but he's not alone."

Cyril focused his gaze further up the street and said, "I haven't seen the man with him before. He's tall and looks a little like a Schnauzer. You should see his mustache."

"Really?" With a leap developed from years of practice, the stubby-legged dog landed on the couch and joined his friend at the window. He carefully edged closer to the open window for a better peek while watching his balance. If he stretched too far, he could tumble off the couch and be punished for climbing on the furniture. "He's better dressed than the other two. A top hat, not a cap. I don't think there's any Schnauzer in him, but he does have that air about him—confident and aggressive. Not one I would approach without caution."

For the past week, the two had noticed a subtle shift in the air. The first hint had been the sudden activity in Camden House. Their abode shared a wall with the vacant building next door. Urgent whispers and constant cigarette smoke drifted past wallpaper and brick and warned of some impending event—whether good or bad, they had yet to determine.

Even more disturbing, however, was the activity across the street. Dormant even longer than Camden House, 221B suddenly had come to life after three long years. Curtains rustled. Footsteps echoed up the seventeen steps to the apartment on the second floor. And now *the man* was back, having appeared the night before, sitting at long stretches at the window, his silhouette showing through the curtains.

"All three of them are conversing now," Cyril said. He continued to watch the three men below them on the street. "I wonder what they are saying?"

"I might be able to find out."

With another accomplished leap, he sped across the room and yipped through the doorway. The maid they called Millie appeared. His response was a flurry of tail wagging and eager jumps at her skirt and apron.

"Good heavens, Ezra," she said, pushing the dog down. "Fancy a stroll so urgently?" A similar round of tail wags and several spins in a tight circle followed. "Let me fetch the leash."

When she disappeared down the hallway, Ezra winked an eye at the cat. "Being a dog does have its advantages."

"Do try to focus out there," Cyril said and licked a paw. "You want to hear what the men are saying? Don't go sniffing at every scent you find."

He hung his head at this reproach. More than once, an enticing aroma had drawn him into trouble. There was the time he was locked in the pantry. Another when he was almost hit by a carriage. He stared at his companion. "I can't help my nature. Any more than you could help it when you almost fell out that window."

"You have to agree that bird was annoying," he said with a lift of his chin. "At least he stayed away after that."

Before he could reply, the maid returned, and the two hustled down the stairs. Millie's arm stretched out in front as she tried to keep the dog from pulling her off her feet.

"Hold on," she said in a high-pitched voice. "Are you in that much of a hurry?"

He was. Who knew how long the men would remain conversing on the street? He stopped upon landing in the street and sniffed the soft, spring air. Checking to his right, he saw with dismay only two men remained. Schnauzer man had left. He knew he had to catch up to them. Hear their conversation. But there were so many scents to follow. Wait. A new one coming from across the street. A hint of beeswax, with something else mixed in. Another wax. The lady at 221B must have been dusting. Probably needed in after three years.

A yowl from the window overhead made both Millie and Ezra glance up to where Cyril still perched. He caught the cat's subtle tail twitch, reminding him to head to the corner immediately. Keeping to task, he turned in the direction Cyril had indicated but was jerked to a halt. His collar bit into his throat and cut his bark into a wheeze.

"This way, Ezra," Millie said and turned toward the opposite corner.

He glanced up at his companion as the maid dragged him behind her. Locking his knees, he planted himself as powerfully as possible. The maid, a slight thing with little seniority (why else would she be the one who had to walk the dog?), pulled on his leash and managed to slide him along on his paws a foot or so. Ezra grimaced. The sidewalk's paving stones scraped the bottom of his paws. He hoped Cyril appreciated his sacrifice for gaining this information. With a whine, he turned his head toward the opposite corner.

The young woman threw up her free hand. "All right, have it your way. But you'd better do your business fast. I've got work to do."

Nose skimming above the ground, he pretended to seek the perfect spot for his "business" as he made his way to the corner and the two men from Camden House. Once he detected the acrid sting of the short man's tobacco, he stopped and tipped his head in their direction. His hearing was keen enough that he heard their mutterings perfectly while still half a house away.

"The Colonel says it will happen tonight. I've seen him shoot; he won't miss from this distance, Parker," whispered the short one.

A tug on his leash almost caused him to miss the other's reply.

"Keep it down," the taller said in a hiss sharp as a blade's edge. "You want the whole street to know what we're planning tonight? But once Holmes is out of the picture, there'll be no stopping us."

He sidled to the edge of the building and lifted his leg, hoping they would share more. The two seemed lost in thought, puffing away at their cigarettes and glancing at the window across the street.

Unfortunately, as soon as he finished, another tug pulled him out of range. The last word he heard was "air." All the way back to the house, he sniffed at the air, seeking to detect something different, but he could distinguish nothing beyond the usual scents.

"You coming down with a cold?" Millie asked after the fifth sniffle. "I'll have Cook make you some pepper tea."

He raised his head at that threat. The last time they'd forced that mixture on him, it burned from mouth to stomach. Whether he resisted or not, it would be poured down his throat. Perhaps if he kept his head up, the maid would forget about the tea. If she didn't, he could only hope Cyril would recognize yet another sacrifice on his part in their efforts to maintain the security of Baker Street.

Once released, Ezra settled onto his bed by the couch. His throat still stung from the leash, but Cyril wasn't going to let him rest. The cat sauntered to the edge of the couch and hung his head over the edge so they could converse more directly.

"What did you learn?"

He licked the front paw, which was most tender after the maid had dragged him across the pavement. "The taller one's name is Parker." His tongue shifted to the other front paw. "Schnauzer man's name is Colonel."

The cat's back ruffled slightly, a sure sign his annoyance was rising. Ezra suppressed the grin wanting to shape his lips. It was too easy to bedevil him. "That's not a name. That's a title."

"Ok. His *title* is Colonel."

"That's it?"

"They said something about 'air.' But I couldn't find anything in the air...No, wait. I did smell beeswax. From across the street. At 221B. I think someone's been dusting."

"Nothing more?"

The tabby leaned farther over the couch edge. Near enough his paw could reach the corgi's nose. No more teasing the cat. He had a scar on his nose from when he'd gone too far before. Best to give up the rest.

With a sigh, he said, "Whatever is happening, it's tonight; and the Colonel is a good shot."

"Tonight," Cyril said slowly, as if savoring the word. He glanced behind him to the street beyond the window. "It's still several hours before dark. We should get some rest. It may be a late night for us."

Ezra couldn't agree more. Stretching out on the bed, he flipped onto his back, exposing his white belly, and wriggled against its rough surface for a good, old-fashioned scratching.

Soon, he was racing down Baker Street, baying as he followed Parker and the Colonel over the cobblestones. His stubby legs had amazing speed, and he was gaining on the two. Their heels were almost within reach. They smelled like...pepper?

With a jerk, he awoke to find Millie, the butler Parkhurst, and Cook all standing over him. His dream faded from triumph to terror. Cook held a bowl in her hands. They'd come to administer the pepper tea.

"Don't fight it," Cyril said from his place on the windowsill.

A lump formed in the corgi's throat. "You have no idea what it's like. Last time, I couldn't bark for three days."

Parkhurst reached down to grab him, but Ezra was faster. He slipped between the man's legs and headed toward the hallway. His nails clicked and slipped on the polished wood, and he slid as he turned to head down the stairs. The maid and the butler blocked off his descent, and he cowered against the stair's banister, letting out a pitiful whine.

"Come here, Ezra," the butler said. His big hands wrapped around the corgi's midsection. "Hand me that blanket, Millie."

Soon he was swaddled tight, a metal tube in his mouth, and pepper tea trickling down his throat.

Don't fight it? Cyril should get a treatment just for giving that advice.

Once enough Cook decided the dose was sufficient, he was released to hobble back to his bed, hacking all the way. In a raspy voice, he told the cat, "Don't talk to me."

The tabby licked his paw and swiped it over his face. "Fine. I won't tell you what I saw when they were giving you the tea."

"What?" He managed to choke out.

"*The man* moved."

"Of course he did. He does have legs."

"But it was *how* he moved. Just turned a bit."

As much as he didn't want to admit it, this observation did intrigue him. The dog pushed himself up from his bed. It took him two tries to get onto the couch. His thwarted escape attempt had sapped his energy.

"See," the cat said. "He was facing that corner. Now he's facing the other. I *saw* it. He rotated. Chair and all."

The corgi had to admit it was rather odd, but all humans did strange things. He was tired, and the pepper had unsettled his stomach.

He burped. "Lying down."

"I'll keep the watch and let you know if I see anything. If it's happening tonight, we must be prepared."

Cyril stretched out on the sill, the late afternoon rays still caressing his back. "By the way, Parker is in a doorway. If I hadn't watched him, I wouldn't know he was there."

Ezra grunted in response, the pepper tea still burned. This change in routine meant something. He knew it. With some effort, he rasped out, "What do you suppose it means? Leaving him alone like that?"

The cat flicked his tail lazily from side to side, his eyes fixed on the scene outside the window. "We know something is happening tonight. They said so. Perhaps this is part of the preparation." He jerked his head and stared out the window. "The man across the street just moved again. Now he's facing toward the corner where Parker is. Do you think he's watching him, too?"

The dog's stomach rumbled, and he shifted on his side in hopes of a little relief. If he were called upon to act, he feared he couldn't do it. He needed rest. "Maybe. I'm going to sleep. You let me know of any changes."

As evening descended upon the quiet street, Ezra drifted in and out of a fitful sleep, trapped between wakefulness and dreams. The pepper tea continued to make his head swim and his stomach churn. As the gaslights were lit and a cool breeze passed through the window, he finally fell into a deep, relaxed sleep.

After what seemed only a second, someone called his name.

"Ezra."

His stomach finally calm, he rolled onto his other side to return to the dream he'd been having about chasing squirrels.

"Ezra!"

He covered his eyes with his paws. Sleep. He needed sleep.

Ten needles dug into his back, and he yelped. Rising to his feet, he wiggled his body to throw off the weight now clinging to him.

Cyril yowled when he flew to the floor. The two faced each other nose-to-nose.

"Why did you attack me? I was finally feeling better."

The cat took on an offended tone and twitched his tail. "You said to let you know if any changes happened. Well, they have."

"The man's moved again?" They had already observed the man doing so on a regular basis. Not something to lose sleep over.

"Yes, but that's not all. There are *more* men in doorways. And—"

"Hush."

"Don't you—"

Ezra growled. "Quiet. There's someone next door."

"But Parker hasn't moved. No one's come near the building. I've been watching."

"Well, then they came in the back. They haven't been here before. One keeps saying 'Watson.' I suppose that's one of their names."

"Watson." Cyril repeated the name as if trying to recall if he had heard it before. "Do you recognize the voices?"

"It's been a long time, but yes. The two men who live across the street."

The cat tilted his head as if considering the information. "Stay here."

With a graceful leap, the cat returned to his post on the back of the couch. "It can't be. The tall one is still in the window."

"I'm telling you it's the same man. You don't think I can't recognize a voice."

"It *is* through a wall—"

"Quiet," the corgi barked. "Someone else is coming. I recognize the footsteps. It's the Colonel."

Ezra cocked his head, straining to hear what passed in the house next door. Some shuffling, maybe. A click. A pop, then…the street's ordinary sounds were shattered by a splintering of glass.

The dog jerked his head up to the back of the couch where his companion stood, back arched, tail straight. "What was that?"

"Something pierced the window and pushed the man down."

A whistle split the street's muffled nocturnal sounds and Ezra's thoughts. Blood pounded in his head, unsettling his stomach once again.

"The whistle's coming from the house next door," Cyril said to no one in particular.

Ezra raised his ear closest to the wall shared with the adjacent house. "There's a great deal of activity next door. Do you suppose they are related?"

"What do you hear?"

"Hold on. Lestrade…Holmes…Molesy…Colonel…fiend…Shikari… Von Herder…arrest…murder…Ronald Adair. Apparently, the one they call Colonel tried to hunt the one they call Holmes."

"Hunt, did you say? I suppose if they were both in the same room, one could attack another—"

"No. No. Although they did do that, too. The broken window and the man across the road. The Colonel did that. And the others didn't like it at all." He raised his head to gaze at the cat. "They are leaving. I want to see them all together."

Despite his comprised state and with great effort, the dog's slightly wobbly legs pushed him onto the couch. He had to pause for a breath or two before he pulled himself onto his back legs and peered onto the street. "Do you recognize any of them?" he asked. "I want to put the voices with the faces."

Cyril raised a paw to indicate the tall, broad-shouldered one. His confident stride echoed through the street as he led a cluster of three up the street. "He visits quite a bit."

"All right, men. We can all head to the station," the one in the lead said.

"That's the one they call 'Lestrade,'" Ezra said. "He was talking to 'Holmes.' Which one is that?"

"The taller of the two crossing the street. The one with him they call Watson."

Ezra studied the back of the tall, lean man dressed all in black. He had some difficulty picking him out from among the shadows, but his erect stature and assured gait counterbalanced his companion's shorter, athletic build to form a most congenial pair.

The street emptied. A large, black-boxed carriage where they put the Colonel clattered away. The shadows of the other two men now replaced the previous solitary figure in the window across the street. A woman's shadow joined them.

"I've missed this view into the room," Ezra said. "They remind me of us, in a manner."

"How so?"

"Just that they appear to suit each other."

"Do you think we complement each other?"

"You see what I cannot. I hear what you don't."

"Hmm." Cyril's thoughtful acknowledgment ended abruptly. He leaped to his feet and settled into a stance the dog knew all too well: a cat on the hunt.

"What is it?"

"Remember the one they called Parker? He suddenly appeared from the shadows. He was helping the Colonel to hunt Holmes."

Ezra studied the figure slipping down the street. "He's coming this way. Perhaps he plans to hunt Holmes like the Colonel. We must stop him. Warn Holmes he is still in danger."

"Stop him? How?"

"Jump. Jump on him. I'll bark and alert them."

"Jump? Do you know how high it is? Besides, you can't bark. They gave you the pepper tea."

"It's not such a terrible height. And I'll bark. I promise. Even if it's the last bark I ever do."

Cyril studied the man not too far from where they sat. Ezra saw him swallow. The corgi dropped back down to the couch seat. Cyril glanced behind him. "Where are you do—?"

The dog set his nose against the cat's body and shoved. He then popped back to a standing position and watched his friend claw the air as he fell directly onto Parker's head and shoulders. The man yelped as the cat's claws sought purchase.

The next part fell to Ezra. With all his might, he took a deep breath and let out a…squeak.

No, he had to do better. The man was pulling on poor Cyril. In a moment he'd be free of the cat and free to hunt Holmes. If a bark wasn't possible, what about…? He took in an even deeper breath and howled. The sound sliced through the street's now peaceful night. Even Parker paused his efforts to extract himself from Cyril's grip.

It also drew the three in the building across the street to the window. The two men disappeared from sight as Ezra continued to howl (although it was quickly dropping in volume), and Cyril to yowl. The cat yelped when Parker managed to grab him by the scruff of his neck and fling him to the pavement.

The commotion drew the residents from all the nearby buildings, and soon they encircled the three. Another of those brain-splitting whistles followed.

Ezra sifted through the crowds' jumbled murmurs of "Holmes," "Reichenbach," and "Moriarty" as a man with brass buttons and a tall hat confronted the three at the center.

"Mr. Holmes?" he asked in a shocked voice. "But-but you're *dead*."

"I'm afraid rumors of my death were greatly exaggerated." He glanced down at Cyril, who had wrapped himself around his leg, and then up to Ezra, who still peered out the window. "I would request that you please take this fellow into custody and deliver him to Inspector Lestrade. His name is Parker. I have been observing him along with Colonel Sebastian Moran for weeks now. He is an accomplice to my attempted murder tonight."

"Accomplice to your murder?" Brass-buttons' voice held more than a little skepticism.

"*Attempted* murder. Lestrade will explain it all." He glanced into the crowd and pointed to a young woman.

Millie covered her mouth with her hands. "I didn't do anything, Mr. Holmes."

"Of course you didn't, but I believe this is your cat."

"Yes. That's Cyril. How did you know?"

"The hairs on your apron. You really must be more careful when you dust."

She glanced down at her apron and turned to point up at the corgi. "That's not Cyril's hair. It's Ezra's. We had to give him some pepper tea for his cold, and it took three of us to hold him down."

The man glanced up at the dog in the window and saluted the animal. "Quite a pair, these two. Because of them, we have Moran's accomplice. All because that dog barked, or rather howled."

I SINCERELY HOPE you enjoyed reading *Master of the Art of Detection* as much as I enjoyed writing it. If you did, I would greatly appreciate a short review on Amazon or your favorite book website. Reviews are crucial for any author, and even just a line or two can make a huge difference.

ACKNOWLEDGMENTS

It may take a village to raise a child, but it is also essential to bring a book to life. I thank Steve Mason, the third mate of The Crew of the Barque Lone Star (DFW Sherlockian chapter), who has been editing a chapter anthology for several years now. His call for mysteries each year inspired some of the stories in this volume. Similarly, submission requests from David Marcum and MX Publishing also inspired some stories. Of equal importance has been the editing advice I've received from Claudia Rose and Nancy Alvey. Whenever I've put out the call for their review and comments on a draft, they have answered enthusiastically and provided insights I've always incorporated into the story. Both push me to be a better writer. Finally, I must thank you, the reader. I am thoroughly grateful for you taking the time to purchase, read, and share my book!

I stand forever in the debt of this village.

ABOUT THE AUTHOR

Liese Sherwood-Fabre knew she was destined to write when she got an A+ in the second grade for her story about Dick, Jane, and Sally's ruined picnic. After obtaining her PhD from Indiana University, she joined the federal government and had the opportunity to work and live internationally for more than fifteen years. After returning to the states, she seriously pursued her writing career.

Award-winning author and member of the prestigious Baker Street Irregulars, she has pursued a writing career for more than thirty years, garnering numerous awards for her pieces, including a Pushcart Prize nomination, and several CIBA awards for her mysteries, essays, and middle-grade fiction.

She loves to hear from her readers, and you can follow her through her newsletter (https://sendfox.com/liesesf), Facebook (http://www.face book.com/liese.sherwoodfabre?ref=stream), X (Twitter) (https://x.com/ lsfabre), and Bookbub (https://www.bookbub.com/profile/liese-sher wood-fabre)

ALSO BY THE LIESE SHERWOOD-FABRE

An Unconventional Holmes
The AudioBook

Missing boys, an imposter husband, and a bizarre vampyre murder.

Sherlock Holmes ventures into the realm of the unnatural in these three cases: the disappearance of the Baker Street Irregulars, the true identity of a Great War veteran, and a vampyre's grisly death. Crossing into the worlds of the Grimm Brothers and Bram Stoker, he seeks the clues needed to unravel the mysteries confronting him. Can Holmes' conventional methods still function in the unconventional world?

Only Sherlock Holmes can save his mother from the gallows

Violette Holmes has been accused of murdering the village midwife. The dead woman was found in the garden, a pitchfork in the back, after a public argument with Mrs. Holmes. After being called back from Eton because of the scandal surrounding the arrest, Violette tasks Sherlock with collecting the evidence needed to prove her innocence. The village constable will stop at nothing to convict her. Can Sherlock save her from hanging?

Turn the page to read the first chapter or scan the code below to find the book at your favorite bookseller.

THE ADVENTURE OF THE MURDERED MIDWIFE

EXCERPT

They told me the Battle of Waterloo was won on the playing fields of Eton, and I knew I should have been honored to be at the institution; but at age thirteen, I hated it. The whole bloody place. I remained only because my parents' disappointment would have been too great a disgrace to bear.

My aversion culminated about a month after my arrival when I was forced into a boxing match on the school's verdant side lawn. I had just landed a blow to Charles Fitzsimmons's nose, causing blood to pour from both nostrils, when the boys crowding around us parted. One of the six-form prefects joined us in the circle's center.

After glancing first at Fitzsimmons, he said to me, "Sherlock Holmes, you're wanted in the Head Master's office. Come along."

Even though I'd been at the school only a few weeks, I knew no one was called to the director's office unless something was terribly wrong. I hesitated, blinking at the young man in his stiff collar and black suit. He flapped his arms to mark his impatience at my delay and spun about on his heel, marching toward the college's main building. I gulped, gathered my things, and followed him at a pace that left me puffing to keep up.

I had no idea what caused such a summons. If it had been the fight, surely Charles would have accompanied me. I hadn't experienced any controversies in any of my classes, even with my mathematics instructor. True, earlier in the day I'd corrected him, but surely it made sense to point out his mistake? For the most part, the masters seemed pleased with my answers when they called on me.

I did have problems, however, with most of my classmates—Charles Fitzsimmons was just one example. Except he was the one who'd called me out. Surely, *that* couldn't be the basis of this summons?

Once inside, my sight adjusted slowly to the dark, cool interior, and I could distinguish the stern-faced portraits of past college administrators, masters, and students lining the hallway. As I passed them, I could feel their judgmental stares bearing down on me, and so I focused on the prefect's back, glancing neither right nor left at these long-dead critics. A cold sweat beaded on my upper lip as I felt certain something very grave had occurred, with me at the center of the catastrophe. Reaching the Head Master's office, I found myself unable to work the door's latch, and with an exasperated sigh, the prefect opened it for me and left me to enter on a pair of rather shaky knees.

My agitation deepened when I entered and found the director examining a letter with my father's seal clearly visible. He glanced up from the paper with the same severe expression I'd observed in his predecessors' portraits. Dismissing his appraisal, I concentrated on the details I gathered from the missive in his hand.

Taking a position on an expansive oriental carpet in front of his massive wooden desk, I drew in my breath and asked, "What happened to my mother?"

"How did you know this involves your mother?" he asked, pulling back his chin.

"The letter. That's my father's seal." My words gathered speed as I continued. "It doesn't bear a black border, which means at least at this point no death is involved. My father's hand is steady enough to write, so he must be well, that leaves only some problem with my mother."

The man raised his eyebrows at my response, then glanced at the letter in his hand before tossing it onto the desk's polished surface. "As you have surmised, a problem at home requires your return. Your father has requested that we arrange for you and your things to be sent to the rail station. Your brother will be arriving from Oxford to accompany you the rest of the way."

My heart squeezed in my chest, dread rushing through my body. Home. Underbyrne, the family estate. And not just for a short visit. Packing all my things meant I was leaving for the remainder of the term. Something terribly wrong had happened. Grievous enough to pull Mycroft out of his third year of studies at Oxford. Blood *whooshed* in my ears, and I barely heard what followed.

"I've already requested Mrs. Whittlespoon to assist you in your packing." Head Master turned his attention to the rest of the mail on his desk. He glanced up to add, "She'll be in your room already."

"Thank you, sir. Good day, sir." I recovered enough to respond to his statement, but not to ask the reason behind Father's directive.

With a wave of his hand, I was dismissed before I could inquire. As I closed the door behind me, I heard him mutter, "As much a prig as his brother."

For a moment, I considered opening the door and requesting more information about his assessment as well as what else my father had provided in his letter, but social convention restrained me from questioning an elder—and the Head Master at that. I was left to ponder my unspoken concerns as I returned to my chamber.

By the time I arrived at my room, my trunk had already been brought down from storage, and Mrs. Whittlespoon, the house dame, was placing my belongings in it.

"There you are, dearie." She pointed to a set of clothing on my bed. "You go change into your traveling clothes while I finish this up."

I paused, considering for a moment to ask her what she knew of the events surrounding my departure, but she had turned her attention to the drawer with my undergarments. Having lost the opportunity for the moment, I retrieved the clothes and carried them to the bathing facilities.

Since the Head Master was not forthcoming, and Mrs. Whittlespoon might have only limited knowledge, my best hope for additional information as to what had occurred with Mother would be Mycroft—if he was in the mood to share. Knowing my brother, he might not be inclined to discuss this or any other matter on the journey home. He'd been overjoyed to return to university after the summer's break and pulling him out would definitely sour his mood.

Mrs. Whittlespoon turned to me when I re-entered the room and placed both her hands on my shoulders for a moment to scrutinize my appearance.

"You look a right proper young gentleman." She smoothed out the sleeves of my coat. "You go on down to the carriage, now. I'll finish up here and have Jarvis take the trunk down to the carriage. I assume you'll want to carry *that* yourself."

She waved her hand at my violin case lying on the bed. A wave of guilt swept over me. At my mother's insistence, I'd begun lessons two years before and developed some skill on the instrument. Since entering Eton I hadn't found the time to practice as promised. How could I report such a failure to her? I swallowed as my next thought rose, unbidden. Assuming, of course, she was in a position to ask—or understand—my answer.

No sooner had I taken a seat in the awaiting carriage, resting the violin case on my lap, than a loud clomping at the dormitory door announced the arrival of my trunk. The handyman's back bent low, and he knees splayed outward. The driver helped him take it the final yards to the rear of the carriage with Mrs. Whittlespoon following behind, shouting orders all the way.

"Mind how you secure it. I didn't spend all that time laying things neatly just so—here now, watch that strap."

The vehicle rocked as the trunk was fastened on. When the movement ceased, Mrs. Whittlespoon stuck her head in the window and passed me a small basket. "Something in case you get hungry on the way."

I bobbed my head. "Thank you. It's quite kind of you."

Before either of us could say more, the driver gave a shout, and the house dame stepped back only a second prior to the carriage jerking forward.

Throughout the trip to the station, I turned over in my mind what little I had gleaned from my exchange with the Head Master. I had assumed the issue lay with her health— although I knew her to be quite hale for a woman of forty- six. What other situation would cause my father to pull both his sons out of school? Scandal possibly. Although, she came from a good family with a stalwart reputation, and my mother was by nature a moral upright person. The most shocking character on either side of her parentage was my grandmother, the sister of Horace Vernet, the artist. Being French and having the patronage of Napoleon III certainly raised eyebrows in some corners, but that would hardly create a scandal worthy of removing Mycroft and myself from school.

The basket Mrs. Whittlespoon had given me bumped my elbow. To distract myself from the thoughts swirling about my head, I took the opportunity to check its contents. A small apple, two thick slices of bread, and a medium wedge of cheese. I found the thought of food unsettling and closed the basket.

Soon after the driver deposited me and my trunk on the station platform, a train pulled in spewing a cloud of smoke and dust. I spotted my brother leaning from the window of a first-class compartment at the rear of the train. He pointed to a man pushing a cart toward me, and once free of my baggage, I joined him.

My brother and father were "cut from the same cloth"—as they say—with thick waists and high foreheads. One had only to examine my father to know how Mycroft would appear thirty years hence. The exception being the eyes. Not in color, but in sharpness. My father's lacked the keen intellect apparent in my brother's. While Father was quite an accomplished man—as a squire he served as a justice of the peace and was versed in many subjects, espe- cially entomology—Mycroft's intensity marked him as our progenitor's intellectual superior.

That keenness also gave him little patience with others. Despite being my only sibling, I was never truly comfortable around him. With rare exceptions, I guarded my words and actions carefully in his presence, knowing they would be weighed, and mostly likely found lacking in some aspect. For that reason, when he indicated I should sit in the tufted, blue seat opposite him in the compartment, I didn't argue. He had taken the backward-facing middle seat because it was less prone to the smoke and dust blown in through the window .

I plopped down on the cushion, and a small cloud of ash rose from my action, sending me into a brief coughing fit. When a small smile graced his lips, I ignored it and settled Mrs. Whittlespoon's basket next to me.

Mycroft jutted his chin at it. "What's that?"

"Mrs. Whittlespoon gave it to me. For the trip."

"What'd she give you?"

"You want it? I can't—I'm not hungry."

He took the proffered basket and studied the contents.

Putting the cheese between the two slices of bread, he took a bite and caused my stomach to flip yet again. It hadn't quite settled when the train lurched forward and another wave of nausea swept over me.

To distract myself, I stared out the window at the passing countryside and summoned the nerve to ask him what had occupied me for the past several hours. "What exactly happened to Mother? I know she's not dead, but I have no information beyond that. Is she sick? Dying?"

"She's fine."

"Someone's not, or we wouldn't be called home."

No reply.

"I'm going to find out. Wouldn't it be better for me to

learn it from you now, than when we arrive at Underbyrne?"

Through his cheese sandwich, he said, "You want to know, you little twit? Here it is. Mother's in gaol, accused of murder ."

The force with which this pronouncement hit me was the same as if he'd given me a blow to the stomach. The queasiness I'd battled since my fight with Fitzsimmons returned with a vengeance. Bile surged into my throat. The compartment closed around me, and my deepest desire was to flee. I stood, realized there was truly nowhere to go, and dropped back down into my seat.

"Put your head between your legs."

I glanced at Mycroft, but his words sounded as if I were under water.

"Put your head between your legs."

When I remained immobile, he grabbed me by the hair and bent me over.

"Breathe," he said.

After several gulps of air, my hearing improved, and my heartbeat slowed. "You can let go now."

He sat back, and I raised my head. "Mother? Wha— How?"

"I don't know all the particulars. I gleaned it from my own analysis of the information in the papers."

He pulled part of a newspaper out of his breast pocket and passed it to me. Despite the train's movement, my original agitation subsided enough for me to read the dispatch concerning Mrs. Emma Brown having been found dead on our estate.

"Mrs. Brown, the midwife?"

Mycroft nodded. The whole village knew the thin, older woman. She'd been at the delivery of at least half the town. The other half had been seen either by Dr. Farnsworth, the village doctor, or Mr. Harvingsham, the village surgeon. As far as I knew, Mother had little contact with Mrs. Brown. Dr. Farnsworth or Mr. Harvingsham tended us during certain severe illnesses, but my mother relied mostly on her own knowledge of herbs and medicine to treat our ailments.

He then handed me another newspaper sheaf. This one was from a larger paper and included an editorial decrying the bias in some county judicial systems. In point, the author noted a recent incident of a justice of the peace's wife whom a local businessman had accused of his wife's murder and yet the woman still resided at home.

"You believe that this refers to Father?"

"How many dead bodies do you think crop up on the property of justices of the peace? Of course, it's referring to our parents, idiot. And after that editorial appeared, the constable was forced to arrest Mother and put her in gaol."

Calmed by the supplied information instead of my own dire speculations, I returned the two papers to him and contemplated this new turn of events. One didn't argue with Mycroft or his ability to deduce specifics from the barest of details. He had exercised his ability to knit together bits of intelligence from various sources into a whole truth for as long as I'd known him. And he was seldom, if ever, proved wrong.

All the same, one glaring omission remained.

"She's innocent," I said.

"I lack enough information to make that assertion."

Mycroft pulled the apple out of the basket. "You sure you don't want this?"

When I shook my head, he bit into it and then spit out what he had in his mouth. I could see the apple's brown inside from across the compartment. Had the circumstances been different, I might have found this comeuppance amusing. Instead, I found no satisfaction in the event, not being able to shift my focus from the idea of Mother as a murderess. Unable to conceive of her in those terms, I returned to my original contention that she had been unjustly accused. And I had to find out what had truly happened—which only Mother could supply.

At that moment, I resolved to find a way to visit her.

I knew where the gaol was. The old, square building sat on a corner near the edge of the village center. Did one simply knock on the door and ask to see a prisoner, as when calling upon a neighbor?

While I wanted to ask Mycroft about the process, he'd already rested his head back against his seat, his eyes closed. I tried to follow my brother's example but found myself unable to rest. I kept imagining my mother locked in a dank cell and found the only way to keep the vision away was to watch the green countryside pass by my window until dusk fell and all that remained was my own reflection staring back.

Father stood on the station platform when we arrived. He said little in greeting other than, "Simpson's waiting with the cart and the footman. Have them bring your trunks out."

Before either of us could respond, he spun about on his heel and left us to follow him.

Once on the road to Underbyrne, I considered raising the issue of visiting Mother, but knew better than to bring up the discussion in front of a servant. Even one as trusted as our steward, Mr. Simpson. The tall, thin man had been with the Holmes family since before my parents married. Given the lack of safe, conventionally acceptable topics to discuss (somehow the weather and the train ride seemed too mundane in the present situation), we rode the hour to the manor house in silence.

When we pulled up to the front door, the familiarity and *sameness* of Underbyrne held me in my seat for a moment. I saw no change in the red-brick structure with its white-framed gabled dormers on the third floor. Nothing suggested anything out of the ordinary had occurred within. Even the sight of Mrs. Simpson in her usual coffee-brown dress standing stiff-backed under the entrance's covered porch appeared normal.

Only when Father said, "Get a move on," did I stir and retrieve my violin case from beside me on the seat and follow the others inside.

"Welcome home, boys," Mrs. Simpson said. Her strained voice was the first indication of the pall over the house. "Your rooms are ready. Mr.

Simpson will bring up your trunks directly. Are you hungry? I had Cook prepare plates of cold meat for you."

I shifted my feet, somehow unable to move farther into the entryway. I glanced about at the all-too-familiar surroundings, seeking some solace in them. In the candlelight, everything had a sort of gilded edge to it, giving off a sense of normalness otherwise lacking in everyone's mood. The entry hall, open to the second floor and lined with three generations of Vernet paintings and the stairway on the right leading to our bedrooms, hadn't changed. Neither had the doors leading to Father's library and office on the right or the parlor and sitting room to the left. The grandfather clock between the two rooms on the left marked the time as it always had.

I glanced at the time. That late was it?

Even the scents of wax and lemon oil said, "home," but I found myself as ill-at-ease as in a stranger's residence.

Ignoring—or perhaps unaware—of my discomfort, Father spoke to me over his shoulder as he passed on to the dining room. "Leave your case in the library before joining us."

Once I was alone with Mrs. Simpson, she held out her hand. "Pass that to me, Master Sherlock. I'll take it up to your room if you wish."

"Is my uncle about?" I asked, handing over the violin.

Her mouth turned down. "He's terribly upset about your mother, you know. He's been keeping to himself for the most part, taking his meals in his workshop. If you like, after you eat, you can take a plate to him. I'm sure he would enjoy a visit from you. Go on now and have a bit of supper. Your moth—" She stopped herself and swallowed hard. "God bless her. She'd want you to keep up your strength, so you could put on the brave face needed at a time like this."

I shifted the weight on my feet. Nothing in the many lessons my father had imparted provided me with the appropriate response for "a time like this." I knew which piece of silver to use with which course, the polite greeting for the different classes of people, and proper dinner conversation; but how did one comport oneself when one's parent faced the possibility of hanging?

Both men were already at the dining table deep in silent contemplation over their meal of cold roast beef and potatoes. I slid into my chair and stared at the thinly sliced meat and potatoes, both with a slight sheen of fat covering them. My earlier repulsion toward food returned, and a lump formed in my throat. Knowing nothing solid would make it past, I sipped the glass of milk beside it.

"Aren't you hungry?" Mycroft asked.

Father lifted his head and studied me for a moment before saying, "You need to keep up your strength, son."

I poked the meat with a fork. Bile threatened my throat again. "What do you suppose Mother is eating?"

He shook his head. "Outside of what we've provided, I suppose whatever they serve her."

"And what's that? Has she told you?"

"I haven't seen her." That statement drew stares from both me and Mycroft. He placed his fork and knife onto his plate before speaking. "It's not that I don't want to. She's forbidden it. The only one she's allowed to see her is Ernest."

"Why our uncle?" Mycroft asked.

I, too, was surprised with her choice. While her younger brother was terribly devoted to her, for all the time I'd known him, he'd actually been more reliant on her than the other way around.

My father merely shrugged. "Her instructions were explicit. I was not to try and visit her, but to send Ernest instead."

"Did she say anything about us?" I asked. "Might I visit her?"

Barely were the words out of my mouth before he responded with a sharp, "No. She said only Ernest."

I wanted to argue, but the firm set of his jaw told me not to pursue the matter further. With a final glance at my uneaten food followed by a churning in my stomach informing me to not even consider sending any of it down, I finished the glass of milk and asked, "May I be excused?"

"You're not going to eat that?" Mycroft asked.

When I shook my head, he pulled my food to his place.

I rose to head to the kitchen.

"Where are you off to?" my father asked.

"Mrs. Simpson asked me to take a plate to Uncle

Ernest."

Another shift in the seat. "Very well, but don't stay too long and overtire the man."

In the kitchen, I could see Cook was already preparing a basket for me to carry to my uncle. More of the cold roast beef and potatoes, some bread and butter, and a crock that I was certain contained more milk. Ernest didn't believe in imbibing spirits.

"Finished already?" Cook asked. I nodded. "Good, then. Take this on over to your uncle. I'm sure he'd like to see you." Another bob of the head, and I headed out the back door to the converted barn behind the house. Uncle Ernest had come to live at Underbyrne before I was born. He'd served with the military in Afghanistan, and, as Mother put it, the experience changed him. Tending to keep to himself, he tinkered there on different inventions. For the most part, his devices involved gunpowder and other explosives and new ways of using them to project items toward walls and other objects. More than once, I'd been involved in testing a prototype. Despite several attempts to interest the military in his contraptions, they had never responded to any of his correspondence.

Loud clanging greeted me about halfway through the yard. Whatever he was fashioning involved metal.

The noise masked the arrival of a woman, who startled me as she stepped from the shadows and into my path. Only because her reflexes were quicker than mine did Uncle Ernest's dinner basket not drop to the ground.

"Master Sherlock," she said in a low whisper as she handed it back to me, "I didn't mean to scare you."

"I wasn't frightened. You merely took me by surprise." Now that she was out of the shadows, I recognized her as one of the women who bought my mother's herbs. "Rachel Winston, isn't it?"

A shy smile spread across her face. "How kind of you to remember me."

How could I not? The woman, a maid at Lord Devony's estate, had been married for just over three years and had been coming to see my mother for almost as long. Always for the same thing.

"My mother's not here. Sh-she's—"

"I know. But don't you worry. I don't believe for a minute she had anything to do with Emma Brown's death. Your mother is the kindest, most generous woman I've ever met. The whole village thinks so—at least, them's who know her ."

"Did you want to see my father, then?"

"No, sir. Actually, I was hoping to see you. Do you know what your mother gives me? I'm almost out and..."

Her voice trailed off and both of us glanced toward the greenhouse—my mother's refuge—at the other end of the house.

"I...uh..." How did I explain that while I helped my mother with her plants, the exact nature of their various preparations was not known to me? She had taught me the plants' properties, but I was not privy to the exact proportions or extractions for the concoctions she prepared for "the ladies," as she referred to the village women. "I'm sorry. I don't—"

Her hand flew to her mouth. "Oh, please, sir. I need those seeds. I-I can't have a baby yet." She squeezed her eyes shut and gave a stifled sob behind her hand. "Now with Mrs. Brown gone, the only one left is Mr. Harvingsham, and he won't—"

A sob cut off the rest of her thought. I glanced toward my uncle's workshop and shifted my weight from one foot to the other. Once again, my father's etiquette lessons were failing me. What did one say to a practically hysterical female?

"Please don't cry, Mrs. Winston. I'm hoping to see my mother shortly, and I'll ask her about them. Come back tomorrow night, and I'll let you know if I could determine what she gives you."

She grasped my free hand. "Thank you, sir. Thank you." After turning away from me, she stepped back into the shadows with a whispered, "I'll see you after I get off tomorrow night."

Once she had disappeared, I continued on to my uncle's workshop and knocked on the door. When he didn't respond, I let myself in.

As I stepped inside, Uncle Ernest's shout echoed through the cavernous old barn. "Duck, boy, duck!"